MW00829962

AMERICA'S
PROMISE

BOOKS BY CELESTE DE BLASIS

WILD SWAN TRILOGY
A Wild Hope
A Wild Heart
A Wild Legacy

AMERICA'S DAUGHTER TRILOGY
America's Daughter
America's Wife

AMERICA'S PROMISE

CELESTE DE BLASIS

bookouture

Published by Bookouture in 2021

An imprint of Storyfire Ltd.
Carmelite House
50 Victoria Embankment
London EC4Y 0DZ

www.bookouture.com

Copyright © Celeste De Blasis, 2021

The right of Celeste De Blasis to be identified as the author
of this work has been asserted.

All rights reserved.
No part of this publication may be reproduced,
stored in any retrieval system, or transmitted, in any form or by
any means, electronic, mechanical, photocopying, recording or
otherwise, without the prior written permission of the publishers.

ISBN: 978-1-80019-330-7
eBook ISBN: 978-1-80019-329-1

This book is a work of fiction. Names, characters, businesses,
organizations, places and events other than those clearly in the
public domain, are either the product of the author's imagination
or are used fictitiously. Any resemblance to actual persons, living or
dead, events or locales is entirely coincidental.

BOOK III

THE SOUTH

Prologue

Addie touched her belly, and she thought of life arising out of all the loss and death she'd seen, and it seemed a miracle of survival. She longed for the quickening time to come, when she would feel the baby move, proving the existence of its life.

She needed the company and knowledge of women who had borne children, and the officers' wives would not do. If she remained among them, the details of her pregnancy would be before them, sure to cause speculation about paternity.

Addie thought of Castleton, of being there in Virginia with her aunts, of going back to the place where her mother had been born. She felt as if a circle had been closed with the thought, and she did not doubt the welcome she would receive there.

Her twin brother, Ad, sent a message to their uncle and made arrangements for Addie to travel, though he left it to her whether or not she would tell Uncle Hartley about the baby. None of this was difficult because everyone assumed that Addie had found it too trying to be with the army so soon after her husband's death. The Washingtons were as understanding as everyone else.

Now that she was leaving the encampment, Addie wished she could feel as numb as when she had arrived. Only her driving need to get to Virginia made it possible to say farewell with dignity to so many people she had come to know and admire over the war years. When she had gone to New York in search of Silas, she had believed she would return to the army with or without him, but this was different. Though her friends could not know it, it was unlikely that she would travel with the army or see many of these people again.

But nothing could ease taking her leave of Matilda, Ad's fiancée. Addie had shared some of Harriet's clothes with her when she first arrived at Morristown, and she insisted Matilda accept more now.

Matilda's eyes filled with tears. "Are you sure you do not wish me to come with you?"

"I would like nothing better, but I need you to keep taking care of Ad, Justin and your brother, Luke. And I need you to send me all the news so that I won't feel as if I am in complete exile."

In the end, Matilda accepted the clothes because Addie gave her no option, and likewise the wagon and horses, except for Nightingale, were left in her charge, too. With the sorry state of the roads, Addie knew she would be safer and more comfortable on the mare than jolting along in the wagon.

Ad had planned to be part of her escort to Philadelphia, but Addie persuaded him not to on the grounds that his duties were too urgent and that perfectly reliable traffic was going back and forth with correspondence between Congress and the Army. In fact, she wanted to spare him because too long in the saddle still pained his lame leg. As a final argument, she pled sentiment.

"I would rather say goodbye here than draw it out," she told him.

Since he felt the same way, he agreed.

The night before she left, they shared a supper together with Matilda and Luke, but both McKinnons found reasons to leave the twins alone before the hour grew too late. It seemed perfectly fitting to let all their present concerns disappear as they recalled scenes from their childhood. Their knowledge of the losses they had suffered since then only served to sweeten the memories, and they laughed together, sharing their fondness for the bold, happy children they had been.

As he prepared to return to his quarters, Ad said, "I know it cannot be exactly the same in these times, but I hope my niece or nephew will grow up as well acquainted with joy as we were."

His claiming of her child as kin was, as he meant it to be, a benediction to Addie's heart.

In the morning, Ad and Matilda saw Addie on her way.

"Care well for each other," Addie bade them, holding her tears back.

Long after Morristown had disappeared in the snowy landscape, the image of Ad and Matilda standing together remained bright and clear in her mind.

Chapter 1

Spring 1780

Addie's journey to Virginia from the Continental Army's camp at Morristown paused in Philadelphia for a few days, where she met her Uncle Hartley. She had not needed to elaborate on why she wanted to go to Castleton; her uncle, like the Washingtons, thought anyone with a choice in the matter would want to be in Virginia. Though little more than a year had passed since Addie had last seen him, Uncle Hartley seemed to have aged much more than that as the war continued to take a visible toll on him. He was not yet fifty, but he looked closer to seventy, and at her first sight of him, Addie abandoned all thought of confiding in him about the baby. She knew it was cowardly, but she would let her aunts decide when and what he should be told.

Addie stayed only briefly in the city while her uncle completed her travel arrangements, but lodging again with the Birdsalls gave her an odd sense of being close to Iain. She had to fight the dangerous, giddy urge to mention him. She could imagine the Birdsalls' reaction were she to say, "Remember Colonel Traverne, the Scotsman who took such good care of your house during the enemy's occupation? I know him much better now than I did when I met him in Boston—much, much better."

She discovered her uncle's political concerns had narrowed to one area—making Congress provide adequate support for General Washington and the Continental Army. Pay, food, clothing, bedding, arms, ammunition, and medical supplies for the men, plus horses, oxen, and fodder and care for these animals that the army needed. The lists of necessities ran through his mind in endless torment made more keen by the loss of his son-in-law and the constant knowledge that his sons and nephews were endangered as much by Congress's inadequacies as by the enemy.

Though she knew he wanted the truth, it pained Addie to confirm that the shortages at Morristown continued to be severe.

"The Congress will spend weeks on petty squabbles, yet cannot get something as basic as flour for bread to our soldiers," Hartley fumed.

"You speak of General Arnold's trial?" Addie inquired with interest, for she still had a special sympathy for the man because of the kindness he had shown to her, Ad, and Matilda. The trial regarding his actions while he had been Military Governor of Philadelphia had caused widespread interest due to his stature as a hero. "At least it is concluded now, and he was found innocent of the major charges, guilty of just two lesser ones, and I have not heard that his commission will be affected."

"His commission remains intact," Hartley confirmed. "And General Arnold feels himself vindicated by the outcome of the trial, but I fear he is not giving serious consideration to the public reprimand that is yet to come from the commander in chief. Congress has decreed it, and General Washington will issue it with all possible grace, but I doubt Arnold will accept it in the same spirit. He is a very proud man."

"Do you think he should have been found innocent of all charges?"

Hartley's voice dragged with weariness. "I am not certain of that, but I am sure that we do not have such a surfeit of proficient officers like General Arnold that we can afford to alienate any of them."

It was a telling admission. Before the war, Hartley had believed so absolutely in honesty and honor he would never have countenanced any degree of malfeasance by a man entrusted with public office, but now he was so concerned about the outcome of the war, military prowess mattered more than anything else. It was disturbingly parallel to the situation that had allowed General Lee so much power.

Hartley continued. "Ah, well, Mistress Arnold is expecting their first child any day now, so perhaps that happy event will ease the sting of any rebuke."

Addie resisted the impulse to put her hands protectively over her belly.

Arnold had children from his previous marriage, but that did not mean he wouldn't be pleased about this increase. Addie thought of her father's heartfelt welcome of each new child.

"I have heard the Arnolds are devoted to each other, which is a good thing, for it cannot have been easy for them with all the whispers about her Tory connections. If Arnold had married a known Patriot, mayhap things would have gone more smoothly for him. If you see him, will you give him my compliments? His visit gave Ad great encouragement that he would keep his leg and walk again."

"I will make a point of telling him. The good wishes of friends become particularly precious in times of distress."

She was glad to leave the city behind, but the cold weather had reached southward, and it was a miserable journey to Castleton. By the time she arrived, she was so exhausted, she allowed her aunts to tuck her into bed, and she slept without waking for nearly twenty-four hours.

"Who is that lady?"

"That's your cousin, Addie."

"Can she come an' live with us?"

"She will come to visit us, just as we're visiting her, but she's going to live here for a while."

"How long she goin' be sleepin'?"

"Not any longer," Addie said, opening her eyes. "Good day. You must be Master Randolph James Fitzjohn."

Standing on the step to the high bed, the little boy was leaning on his elbows, his head cupped in his hands, and he was one of the most beautiful children Addie had ever seen, with golden-brown curls, bright brown eyes, a button nose, and a cupid's bow mouth. She saw the shadow of the man, realizing his father must have looked very like this when he was small.

She looked up at Sissy, standing behind him, blonde, blue-eyed, trimly curved, the same and yet so changed from the last time she had seen her. It was impossible to see into one's own eyes in a mirror, but Addie could see herself in Sissy's eyes—aged by war, wary about what further sacrifice would be demanded.

"Welcome home," Sissy said, and both of them blinked back tears, not wanting to distress the child.

He broke the tension by announcing, "I calls me Rand." And then he said, "If I stays in bed too long, it gets wet. Do that happen to you, too?"

He was gratified, rather than affronted, that he had amused the adults.

"It might well happen to me if I lie here laughing," Addie told him.

Sissy looked heavenward, as if seeking assistance, and muttered, "This will be another interesting discussion. I'm not sure I am clever enough to explain why wetting the bed might not be the best topic of conversation in polite company." She shepherded Rand out of the room, leaving Addie to her morning ablutions.

Addie accepted help in dressing when a young maid appeared, as her hands were shaking so much as she rushed to make herself presentable, knowing her aunts would be waiting for her. She knew she could not delay in telling them the truth.

It was reassuring that Catherine and Camille had aged far less than Hartley. It was as if being so fully responsible for the welfare of Castleton in the absence of the men had strengthened them. Sissy, having left Rand to play with some of the slave children, waited with them, and Addie thought that this was surely the company of women she had craved, if they did not shun her after her confession.

She looked at each beloved face, and then she told the truth.

"I have come to you because I am with child. I will raise it as my husband's, but it was fathered by another man, after Silas's death. He did not force me, and were this another time, I would count myself fortunate to become his wife." As much apprehension as she felt saying the words, there was also enormous relief, as if speaking of it aloud added weight and validity to the intensity of the brief affair with Iain.

Her aunts exchanged a look, but neither of them appeared particularly shocked. Catherine, ever the more domestic and maternal of the pair, spoke first. "We thought it must be something of this nature. After all, you have traveled with the army for four years, and your brothers are still part of it. We know you too well to believe that even the tragic death of your husband would be enough to drive you away from Ad and Justin."

"You were right to come to us. This is a fine place for children to be born and raised," Camille said.

Addie wanted to smile at the satisfaction in her aunt's voice. Camille regarded Castleton's young—be they foals, or calves, or children—as worthy of the best care.

But Sissy's reaction stopped Addie's smile. Her cousin's face was set, the blue eyes hurt.

"This man, your lover, he is one of the enemy, isn't he?" She did not wait for confirmation. "How could you do it? How could you lie with one of them? They killed my husband and yours and one of your brothers, and they may yet kill the brothers who remain to us. How could you do it?"

It would have been easier had Sissy attacked her in anger; her hurt and disappointment were far harder to counter, and Addie did not try.

But Camille spoke for her. "Addie's father is 'one of them,' and he is an honorable man. And she has a brother who is also 'one of them.' Likewise, we have friends and neighbors who have never stopped being loyal to the King. It would be much more comfortable if all of our enemies were evil, would it not? But, alas, that is not the case. I think we must trust that Addie would not choose a scoundrel, be he Patriot or Tory, to love."

Sissy was frozen in place. Her mouth worked, and Addie winced as she saw her bite down hard on her bottom lip. "I can't bear it, I can't!" Sissy moaned, and she fled.

"I must go elsewhere. I cannot drive Sissy away from her home." Addie's mind began a frantic reconsideration of possibilities she had already discounted.

Catherine interrupted her thoughts, her serenity unbroken. "You are Lily's daughter; for that reason, and because we love you for your own sake, you will always be welcome here. Sissy's home is Bright Oak now, and she is very busy there, watching over the property that will be Rand's when he reaches his majority. Please be patient with her. She is fleeing from her own truth as much as from yours, but she will be back very soon."

Addie agreed to wait, but inwardly she was resolved to leave if Sissy did not return within a week. Perhaps she could stay in her uncle's

Williamsburg house, or maybe she would have to disrupt Tullia's life after all. The one thing she could not do was to blame Sissy for her attitude; had their situations been reversed, Addie knew she might well have reacted the same way.

Addie spent the next few days exploring Castleton. Cold was delaying the spring, but here and there the first touches of green showed in promise. Hartley's efforts—and Camille's too—before the war to make Castleton more self-sufficient, less dependent on English trade, were proving their worth, for there was no lack of a wide variety of food, no shortage of homespun to clothe everyone.

But there were changes. Many of the older, fully trained horses were gone, in service in mounted units of the Continental Army. And though there were markets for grain and salted fish in the French and Spanish colonies, exporting anything was difficult with British ships prowling the seas. Like most who were ardently supporting American efforts in the war, the Castletons were facing diminishing fortunes by the year.

The slaves greeted Addie with the same deference as they always had, but she found the pervasiveness of slavery at Castleton more disquieting than ever before. The people were well fed, well treated, and clothed, but it was not enough. She thought of one of Washington's former aides, John Laurens's, futile attempt to form Black regiments and grant freedom for service and decided that there must be no greater paradox than having great numbers of slaves in a country that had been created for the sake of independence. And yet, she was part of the paradox, for she was here, accepting comfort provided by slaves.

Her guilt deepened when she told Hebe, one of the slaves who always asked about Tullia, about Tullia's marriage and the birth of her son. Hebe's fierce joy that Tullia's liberty had expanded to include a freedman and a child born free blazed as bright as a flame. In the next moment, it was extinguished, and her expression was as bland as usual. Her own husband, a fellow slave, had been dead for years, and only one of her children, a son, also a slave, remained alive.

Four days after Sissy had fled, she returned with Rand, who greeted Addie with a big grin and outstretched arms. She picked him up and cuddled him, receiving a wet kiss and a giggle of delight.

"It is his fault. He has been unrelenting in his campaign to see you again. I think he is going to propose marriage," Sissy said, her rueful smile not quite covering her worry about seeing Addie again.

"Cousin Azzie, you pretty like Mama," Rand announced, snuggling closer.

Addie gloried in the warm vitality of him. "Thank you, Cousin Rand. You are a gentleman, for your mama is one of the prettiest ladies in the land."

With her usual view to the practical and wanting to give her nieces time alone, Camille appeared to ask Rand if he would like to go with her to the stables to check on a new foal, and the little boy left with her, chattering all the while.

"He's wonderful," Addie said, "and so happy."

"Why shouldn't he be? Here he is adored by his grandmother and his great-aunt; at Bright Oak by James's family; and at both by the servants."

"And by his mother always, anywhere."

"Of course. He is my delight." Sissy's face was tender with love, but then her eyes slid away from Addie's. "I am sorry for my behavior, for being so harsh with you."

"You have a perfect right to—" Addie began.

Sissy stopped her. "No, I don't! Because it really isn't about you, at least not directly. I know it seems crazed, but James died so far away, part of me has pretended the report was a mistake, that he is not dead and will come riding in any day to be with me and Rand again. But you have been with the army, with James, with my brothers and yours, and the truth came with you. My precious husband who loved me so kindly and whom I loved from the time I was too young to know—he is not coming back, not ever." Her voice dropped until Addie had to strain to hear it. "I want to understand, I do. But I thought you loved Silas as much as I loved James, and I don't see…" She plucked nervously at her dress as she struggled to find the words.

"I envy you your untouched memories of James. I cannot remember Silas as he once was, not for more than a few seconds at a time."

And then the words poured out, as if this first admission had broken a dam inside of Addie.

"All the year without him, I imagined him as he had always been to me, so tall and strong, but when he was returned to me, he was so frail, so close to death. I loved him still, but it was as if he had become my child. Even so, I would have done anything to keep him with me. But I wasn't strong enough. I felt him leave me; I saw him buried. For a while I thought I was going to fall into the grave with him because every night, in my dreams, the grave grew more vast until it swallowed the living and the dead. I could see them all; I could smell and taste death. Perhaps it was wrong, what I did, but when I went to Iain, he banished the demons, and he asked for nothing. What I gave him, I gave freely. He was not a stranger to me."

She told Sissy of their history, and of Iain's own, of the loyalty of his men; she told her of his intelligence, strength, honor, and gentleness; she told of it being Iain who had gone aboard the prison hulk and carried Silas out, Iain who had had so much to do with the tender care Silas had received in Darius's house.

"I want Iain's child. I want to raise him or her to be as healthy and joyful as your son."

Sissy let her breath out on a long sigh. "It is a hard thing to say, but you were widowed at Monmouth, not in New York. The war has turned everything upside down, but Aunt Camille is right; we have good friends, friends like your father, who are loyal to the Crown. Your Iain sounds the best of men to me, for he is fighting for the most basic of all things—the safety and wellbeing of his family and the people who depend on them. I regret that he cannot fight for our cause, but I understand."

"You are more generous to him and to me than I am," Addie said, and though she was grateful for Sissy's sympathy, part of her ached that her beautiful, once light-hearted cousin had been forced so early to this maturity.

Sissy was much the duty-bound matron now, for while James's parents were still alive, Catherine had told Addie that the loss of their son had debilitated them greatly, and since Bright Oak would come to Rand, they had relinquished most of the responsibility for preserving the property to Sissy. She also had the care of James's sisters, aged

fourteen and sixteen, as part of her burden. It was much to the good
that Sissy was so fond of the two girls, but she was only twenty-three,
Addie's age, young to act as guardian to them, particularly when the
war had so disrupted normal social life. It wasn't just a matter of many
young men being off with the Continental Army and the militia,
or of limited funds making lavish entertaining a thing of the past;
even the seat of government had been shifted from Williamsburg
to Richmond to place it farther inland, farther from the reach of
raiding parties carried on British ships. It was a profound change,
for Williamsburg, as Virginia's capital, had been the social center for
families like the Castletons and Fitzjohns. Though Richmond was
convenient to Castleton and Bright Oak, being northwest of them
on the James River, Sissy called it "an upstart village" and was sure
that Williamsburg would resume its former importance as soon as
the war was over.

When they spoke of the war, Addie and Sissy were determinedly
positive, speaking of it as if it would end soon in favor of the United
States. But Addie knew her cousin shared her doubts.

With every day, she had more reason to be thankful for Sissy's kindness toward her. Sissy was a good companion, and because they were
the same age, it was easier for Addie to talk to her than to Catherine
or Camille. She looked forward to Sissy's visits to Castleton, and she
spent time at Bright Oak, though the first encounter with James's
family was difficult because she was the last among them to have seen
him alive. She gave them every detail she could, but it was not enough;
she could not bring him back for them. However, after that first tense
encounter, the Fitzjohns welcomed her warmly.

It was not surprising that Sissy was close to her husband's family,
but it startled Addie when Cordelia Wakefield Armacost came to call,
and when Sissy greeted her old nemesis quite cordially. With her pale
skin and black hair, Cordelia was still a stunningly beautiful woman,
but the years had marked her, too. Her planter husband, his children,
and her newborn son had died of fever three years ago, after only two
years of marriage, leaving her in lonely possession of the Armacost
holdings. According to Sissy, there was no shortage of suitors, but

Cordelia was unmoved by their pleas of passion, knowing most of them were more interested in property than in matters of the heart.

"What an odd triumvirate of widows we are," Cordelia said with a hint of her old brittle edge, but it was quickly eclipsed by a rueful smile, and Addie saw the weariness in her and the softness so much loss had brought.

Cordelia stayed for two nights, the Armacost plantation being too distant for quick visits, and Addie felt genuine regret when she left. "Who would have guessed she would prove such pleasant company?" Addie marveled.

"Not I," Sissy admitted. "She used to make me feel like the worst gawk, and I used to fear she was going to snatch James away or capture one of my brothers. I don't know whether Cordelia cared deeply for Richard Armacost when she married him, but she came to love him and his children very much before they died. Their courtship started here, the night James proposed to me. How jealous I was of her in those days. But our separate memories of that night comfort each of us, and Castleton remains a special place to her, though she could not bear to come here for a full year after the deaths. And now I must be on my way, too. Rand was quite cross that he wasn't allowed to come on this visit,"

"Tell him 'Cousin Azzie' will be over soon." She was growing increasingly fond of him, and the easy rapport she had with him gave her confidence in how she would deal with her child.

With the harsh winter finally loosening its grip, the pace of life at Castleton and Bright Oak accelerated. New foals, calves, piglets, chicks, and goslings were arriving, fields needed planting, and there were myriad other tasks required by the advent of spring.

The first green in the fields and woods and the first flowers were so beautiful to Addie, they were almost painful to behold. Every leaf and petal and the voices of every newborn bird and animal seemed to speak of the life she carried, and when she felt the first faint flutters inside, she was filled with such exaltation, she could scarcely contain it, wanting to laugh and cry at once.

She knew that for the time being, she was in the right place for herself and the baby, and yet, there was part of her that longed to be with the army. She missed the music, the fifes and drums that commanded the troops to march and measured the beginnings and endings of the days; the ring of spurs and thump of booted feet as express riders and aides hurried in and out of headquarters; even the boom of guns, no matter the ominous message. Most of all, despite the dust, mud, filth, and general hardship, she missed being part of a great movable community, and when she thought of the troops marching out of winter quarters, she yearned to be with them.

Not wanting them to think her ungrateful, she did not discuss this feeling with her aunts or cousin, but she listened to and read every bit of war news she could obtain. She was aided in this by her uncle, for he regularly sent news of the activities of Congress and the army to his family, and he was most obliging in making sure letters to Addie from her brothers got to Castleton as swiftly as possible.

Her first letter was from Justin, and she opened it with trepidation, but his words were balm to her heart, though the most important lines also made her sad for him, for the dark view the war had forced him to see.

> *I am sorry I did not see you before you journeyed south but not for your reason for leaving us. Ad and Matilda assure me the child you carry already possesses your heart. That is reason enough for me to be a proud uncle to your son or daughter. My dearest sister, I have witnessed and been a part of such savagery in this war, it gives me hope that new, innocent life can begin at such a time.*

A note from Ad, included in Justin's letter, eased her sorrow and made her smile, as it was intended to do.

> *You were right. Hammy has proposed, Betsey has accepted, and her parents approve, though when the marriage will take place is in question. Hammy continues to drift about in a most uncharacteristic state, a man transformed into a mooncalf by love.*

There were further details of camp doings, but little war news in this first letter, but subsequent missives were filled with it, in particular with her brothers' mutual frustration.

The Marquis de Lafayette was back in America with promises that not only naval vessels, but also troops, would arrive soon in the United States. He had been well received on his return to France, in spite of having left in the first place without royal permission. Ad wrote of how happy they all were at headquarters to have the marquis back with them. But even the expectation of additional assistance from France could not outweigh the grim turn the war had taken in the South. On May 12, after weeks of siege, Charles Town fell to Clinton and Cornwallis. The entire defending force of over five thousand Americans, Continental troops and militia, surrendered. Their friend John Laurens was among the prisoners.

No matter how much the event had been anticipated, the enormity of the loss was appalling. With Savannah, Georgia and Charles Town, South Carolina under British control, General Clinton was well on his way to accomplishing his aim of winning the war by conquering from the South northward. And General Washington was still stuck in place, held there by the enemy garrison in New York. On news of a large French fleet heading for American waters, Clinton returned to command in New York, leaving Lord Cornwallis in charge of the Southern campaign.

Addie could not help thinking of Iain and Darius. They had both participated in the Charles Town siege and could still be there with Cornwallis, if they had not gone back north with Clinton as Colonel John Simcoe and his troops were reported to have done. She wanted them to lose the war, but she wanted them unharmed in the process; it was a duality of desire that could not be reconciled.

As the spring gave way to summer, heat blanketed the land, and the crops seemed to grow visibly. Addie felt as if she were part of the general fecundity as her body grew voluptuous with the baby, her once small breasts swelling, her belly rounding out. Only her aunts and Sissy were privy to the true paternity of the child; the servants and visitors such as Cordelia all accepted that Addie's husband had fathered it before his tragic death. But while Addie continued in her determination that the child would be protected by that lie, it was Iain, not Silas, who slipped into her mind when the baby kicked energetically or when she daydreamed about who the child would favor in looks. Clear images of Silas as he had once been remained beyond her reach, but she could see Iain distinctly.

She felt perfectly safe at Castleton, but as the summer wore on, her brothers began to share their growing disquiet with her. Ad wrote: "There is little to stand in the way of Cornwallis should he advance to Virginia. Please consider coming north at least as far as Philadelphia while you are still able." Matilda added a note, saying that she would join Addie in the city, but Addie had no intention of leaving Castleton. She believed the threat was real, but she did not believe that Virginia would fall as readily as Georgia and South Carolina, although North Carolina was not apt to provide much of a barrier against the enemy.

However, it was impossible to deny that a bad situation was yet again being made worse by the Congress. In a futile gesture toward relieving General Lincoln at the siege of Charles Town, Congress, instead of giving it to someone else as worthy as Lincoln, and instead of consulting with General Washington as to the choice, bestowed command of the Southern Department on General Gates, one of Washington's past detractors and a man known to be after the role of commander in chief for himself.

When Ad wrote to his sister, he was too infuriated to be discreet.

> *My God! We thought the man safely stored away with the army in New England where he could do no more harm. Now this, it is intolerable and the worst of insults to His Excellency! And it is dangerous. General Gates is a bad soldier and a worse commander. By now, everyone should know the Victory at Saratoga was not his, but belonged to General Arnold. I, of all people, can understand why Arnold feels obliged to refuse field duty on account of his leg wounds, but it is a bloody shame that it is not he or someone of equal caliber, rather than Gates, who is taking over our beleaguered Southern Department.*

The reprimand of Arnold ordered by Congress had been duly issued by General Washington, and as prickly with pride as Arnold was known to be, few doubted that he had resented it. But Washington had made it clear that he continued to have absolute faith in Arnold as a soldier, no matter what irregularities there might have been in Philadelphia, and when Arnold had declined a field command but requested command of the post at West Point, Washington had done everything he could to secure it for him. The fortifications at West Point were of great importance in control of the Hudson River, vital to the transit of men and supplies between New England and the Mid-Atlantic states. Still, even knowing that, Addie, like her brother, wished that Arnold were heading for the Carolinas rather than watching over the Hudson. There were other officers, too, including most of those who were closest to Washington, who could surely be trusted with the Southern Department—a long list of men, which would not have included the name of Horatio Gates.

Uncle Hartley wrote from Philadelphia, and his fury matched Ad's when he bewailed the idiocy of "civilians who neglect the best military advice in the midst of a war," but Hartley's fear for his family's safety was as great as his anger at what the Congress had done, and he was blunt.

> *If the enemy gets to Virginia, you must be prepared to come north. No property is worth your lives. Given my position with the government and the fact of our sons and nephews serving in the Continental Army, it would be too much to hope that the enemy could mistake our loyalty.*

He continued with a precise list of what preparations they were to make now while there was time and how they were best to remove everything from silver to livestock from the enemy's grasp.

Catherine and Camille shared his advice with Sissy and dutifully did what they could to follow his instructions, but neither had any intention of abandoning the plantation.

"We could not take all our people with us nor provide for them if we could, and we will not leave them," Catherine announced. "My husband means well and is protective of us, but he has been away a long time. Perhaps he has forgotten that Castleton is like a village surrounded by wilderness. We would need our own navy to evacuate everyone. The British have been wooing slaves from their masters since the war began, but they do it only to punish the masters, not to reward the slaves."

Addie wanted to protest that freedom was valuable at any cost, but she could not when she remembered the miserable runaways in New York. They had fled to the Crown's protection and had received only deprivation and death by hunger, exposure, and disease for their trust.

"Of course, we will make sure you and your child are safely away," Camille said, as calm as Catherine. "You do not have the protection of being an old woman."

"I do not regard either one of you as old, but in any case, age has been no proof against attacks by the British and their Hessian henchmen, and I may be safer than you because of my brother Darius. General Clinton thinks highly of him," Addie reminded them wryly. She did not commit herself to staying or to going. She could not imagine leaving her aunts, but then again, she had never before had a child to protect. She doubted the enemy would have time to arrive at Castleton before the baby did.

The French arrival in Newport, Rhode Island, in mid-July was heralded as a sure sign of the improving fortunes of the United States, and the French troops were reported to be dazzling in their crisp, bright uniforms that were such a contrast to the ever shabby appearance of the Continentals. But Newport was a long way from the Carolinas, and it was difficult to see of what immediate practical use the French could be.

Addie wished she could have been there to see them come ashore; she wished she could be with Ad at headquarters—at present located in Preakness, New Jersey—to help with the deluge of French correspondence that had to be translated into English for Washington and most of his officers, after which the replies had to be translated from English into French. Washington and the Comte de Rochambeau, the French commander, and their respective staffs had to arrange cooperation between the French and American forces. But Addie knew, with rueful amusement, that not even a pressing need for French speakers would win her a place at headquarters in her present condition.

She had remained relatively trim and agile during most of her pregnancy, but as the last month approached, she felt as if her body had been taken over completely by the baby. Though her aunts assured her there was little chance of twins, she felt as if her belly was distended enough to hold at least two babies, though it seemed there was only one, kicking and turning and throwing her off balance on a whim. She waddled when she walked, needed help getting up from a chair, and wanted more than anything to be able to sleep on her stomach.

And yet, despite the growing discomfort, she loved being with child. It was a reaction she would never have anticipated. Nor, though she wished Tullia were with her, did she fear delivery; she was sure both she and the baby would come through it in good health. So much had been lost; ransom had already been paid for this infant's life.

More and more, she had come to think of the baby as solely hers, but when she went into labor on a hot August night, and the pain was fierce, she saw Iain, saw his strong face and his deep-blue eyes. And when the child was born with the dawn, she saw a tiny, feminine version of Iain in their daughter, and she named her Johanna Valencourt Bradwell—Johanna, for John, for Iain.

Johanna, from her thick cap of black hair to the pink shells of her toenails, was the most perfect being Addie had ever beheld, and the pull of the rosebud mouth on her breast sent so startling a current of delight through her, she laughed even as she wiped away tears.

During the next days she was so absorbed in Johanna, Addie was aware of little that was going on around her. Sissy came to see the baby and was suitably impressed by her beauty, though Rand was disappointed that his new cousin was so little that it would be a "long, long time till she gets big enough to play." And he was skeptical when his mother insisted he had once been just that small.

When the world around her began to come into focus again, Addie realized something was seriously amiss. Both her aunts seemed distracted, and they didn't quite meet her eyes when she inquired if there was any news of the war. Finally she confronted Camille.

"What is it? Is it the war or do you and Aunt Catherine see something wrong with Johanna that I don't see?"

Camille was so shocked at this idea, the truth escaped her before she could call it back. "No, oh no! Johanna is as perfect as you think she is! It is the war indeed. The enemy may be here sooner than we thought. The day before Johanna was born, General Gates was routed by the enemy at Camden, in South Carolina. His army was very nearly destroyed with many killed or taken prisoner."

Camille gripped her hands so tightly together, Addie could see the bones distending the skin as her aunt went on.

"Everything Hartley and Ad wrote to us of Gates has proven true. The man fled early in the battle, leaving his army behind. He fled to North Carolina, to Charlotte, and on to Hillsborough. He raced nearly two hundred miles in less than four days. Surely with that feat, he outdistanced any faint claim to honor he ever had." Camille took a deep breath. "The land itself may be the best weapon we have left to us. You have never been further south than Virginia, have you?"

Addie shook her head.

"In the Carolinas, particularly in South Carolina, the British will face numerous hazards. In the lowlands in summer there are venomous snakes and insects, suffocating heat, dread fevers, and strange diseases that rot the flesh and will not let the smallest sore heal. There are swamps and impenetrable thickets everywhere and no roads to speak of. It is far more severe than Virginia. Even if they retreat to higher, cooler terrain, our enemies will find vast forests of pine and hardwood on barren ground, providing little forage for men or beasts."

Addie's first burst of panic eased as she considered her aunt's words. They made sense, particularly when she recalled that in New York, the enemy had always had a full complement of soldiers too ill for duty and it had been openly acknowledged that fresh troops arriving from the Old World were at great risk until they were seasoned by surviving for a time in the New World. She could not deflect thoughts of Iain and his men. As hardy as they were and as long as they had been in the United States, nothing in their background in Scotland or in Europe could have prepared them for the wilderness of the Carolinas.

Enraged that Gates had fulfilled their worst prophecies, Hartley and Addie's brothers sent increasingly urgent pleas that retreat from Castleton be contemplated seriously. They also sent congratulations on the birth of Johanna and were not above using her as an added reason for removing to safer ground.

"As if the enemy hasn't been burning down defenseless towns in the North, and as if hauling a newborn infant about is not dangerous in itself," Addie snorted, but she was pleased by the hearty good wishes. She did not ask Catherine what she had written to her husband about the pregnancy, but whatever it was, Hartley wrote to Addie with no hint of shock or disappointment.

Ad relayed the felicitations of his fellow aides and other friends and wrote with blunt kindness:

> *Little Johanna will be warmly welcomed when you return to us. You were wise to go to Virginia, though you must not linger there too long. Justin and I have been vague about how long the news of her birth took to reach us, vague about her birthdate, and there have been no untoward questions or speculations.*

Addie appreciated the efforts of her brothers to protect her reputation and that of her child, but she knew the war was her best ally in this, for it kept people too fixed on their own precarious lives to spare much concern for the doings of others.

Uneasy news drifted out of the Carolinas. Cornwallis was securing outposts in order to control South Carolina, his next obvious need being to take over North Carolina. But he was not unopposed. Patriots attacked British and Loyalist military units whenever and wherever they could, stinging swiftly before they faded back into the undergrowth. They could not stop Cornwallis, but they would slow him down.

The internecine strife in South Carolina was bitter, especially on the western frontier, and small groups of Patriots and Loyalists went at each other at every opportunity, in spite of having been closely bound together by kinship, friendship, and commerce before the war had made the difference between a Whig and a Tory more important than any mutual interests.

With mingled hope and frustration regarding joint action, Ad wrote from Hartford, Connecticut, on September 22, about Washington's first meeting with the Comte de Rochambeau. Ad had gone with Hammy and other aides and with Lafayette, Knox, and other officers in Washington's suite.

> *My ability to speak French is more important at present than my inability to walk with grace. I wish I had time to describe at length the festivities here, for we have been met with great ceremony by the local military, state officials, and the citizenry. His Excellency has been hailed with hearty cheers and the salute of guns at every opportunity. And Rochambeau seems an impressive, intelligent gentleman. Unfortunately, the British fleet continues to lurk outside of Newport, and there is no sign of the French fleet, so any activity by the French troops must be severely limited.*

Addie did not receive his letter until the second week of October. It arrived enclosed in a letter written later by Hartley to all of them, and the news was so dreadful, it was nearly impossible to believe.

> *My Dearest Ones,*
>
> *Rumor flees at such a pace, perhaps this news has come to you already. Would that it were only rumor, but it is truth.*
>
> *General Arnold has gone over to the enemy. It seems this business has been transacting for some time, and his intention was to surrender West Point and all the men and magazines*

therein to the enemy. But his British friend, Major John André,
was captured before he could make his way back to his army.
He carried with him the plans to the fortifications at West
Point, and he was out of uniform, dressed as a civilian. André
was held fast, but Arnold escaped and is now in New York.
General Washington would have traded André for Arnold, but
General Clinton would not agree. It is an uneasy business, but
I believe there was no choice. After a court martial, André was
hanged as a spy. Many of our soldiers who witnessed it wept
openly, for André was said to be a man of charm and wit who
died with great courage. His last words were, "I pray you bear
witness that I meet my fate like a brave man." Would that the
noose had been around Arnold's neck. No tears would then
have fallen. I wish the man swiftly in hell.

As Catherine read the letter aloud, Addie felt more queasy than she ever had during her pregnancy. She felt as if the very earth had become unsteady. General Arnold, "gone over to the enemy"—the words echoed over and over in her head. Arnold the hero of Saratoga, the valorous Patriot, Arnold the traitor, Arnold the betrayer, Arnold who had been so kind to her and Ad and Matilda. She could not reconcile the disparate images. She thought of the sharp-eyed Major André, handsome, urbane, artistic, and so dangerously intelligent; all of that life dispatched by a twist of rope. She had feared him because of her own secrets, but that he had been executed while Arnold had gotten away without injury was intolerable.

"I have met both of them," she mumbled, and she explained the circumstances. "Poor General Washington, he had such faith in Arnold, his heart must be sorely wounded. And Major André was so high in his favor, General Clinton will be grief-stricken. André was too clever to be easily caught. I doubt not that Arnold had much to do with his downfall."

The tale of treachery and woe worsened with further details from Ad. For truly, André had had no intention of being out of uniform in American territory, but when the British ship, the *Vulture*, which had been serving as his transport, had been fired upon and had moved out of reach on the river, André had been stranded. Instead of involving himself in the difficult task of securing a boat to row André back out to the *Vulture* as he had been brought from it, Arnold chose the easier course for himself, sending André off on horseback in the company of a guide of dubious intelligence who had been told that André was nothing more than a New York merchant. In this disguise, André had tried by road and ferry to reach White Plains, north of Manhattan. But the land was alive with patrols of Cowboys and Skinners, and left alone to ride the last fifteen miles to White Plains, André was stopped on the Tarrytown Road. Thinking he was in an area controlled by Tory Cowboys, he made his fatal blunder, identifying himself as a British officer on important business. The men he faced were Patriot Skinners, and miserable lot though they were, they did not accept his offer of bribes, for he had no money with him, and they probably feared that once he reached his lines, a British patrol would be sent out after them, or that if they tried to collect on a note, they would be captured and hanged. He had no money, but he did have papers and a pass signed by General Arnold. The Skinners took him to North Castle, the nearest American post.

Lieutenant Colonel Jameson, the commanding officer there, decided the proper course was to send the papers and the prisoner to General Arnold, and they were on their way when Major Tallmadge, who had been on scouting duty, came to the post and heard Jameson's account of this strange business. Tallmadge immediately suspected the truth, for Arnold had made no secret of providing a pass for "John Anderson," and if the man was carrying diagrams of West Point, then the information must come from Arnold. Tallmadge had urged Jameson to order that both André and the papers be brought back to him until more could be learned and to give no warning to Arnold in case he was involved in nefarious business. But Jameson outranked Tallmadge, and though he did send to have the prisoner taken out of reach of British ships and the confiscated papers sent on to General Washington, he insisted that his letter to Arnold still be delivered to him because, after all, General Arnold was his superior officer.

Addie could feel Ad's pain in every careful detail he had written to her, as if he were picking at a wound that would never heal, for he had been there when Arnold had fled. He and the other aides and officers and guards had been part of the large retinue that had accompanied General Washington to the meeting with Rochambeau and had been on their way back to headquarters, with a planned stop to inspect the fortifications at West Point and to visit with General and Mistress Arnold.

> *I was so close, so damnably close! If I had but known, I could have stopped him. We were to breakfast at Beverly, the estate where the Arnolds were staying on the East Side of the Hudson, but as we neared the place, His Excellency decided he wanted to check the redoubts along the way, and he sent me to tell General Arnold not to delay breakfast for his sake. Though Lafayette was hot to be in the presence of the fetching Peggy, the general teased him out of going to Beverly before the inspection was complete. He sent me instead, as a special kindness. We had been traveling a good deal in the past days, and my leg was somewhat swollen, and by sending me to Arnold, the general thought to give me a little extra respite. When I arrived at the house, I was informed that Mistress Arnold was not well, but General Arnold greeted me most cordially. Oh, my dear Addie, the perfidy of the man! He asked after you and Matilda in the kindest manner. And he bid me sit down to breakfast with him and rest my leg. He claimed he was most anxious to meet with the commander in chief and was generous in his praise of him. And I believed every word. I shall never trust my judgment again.*
>
> *In the course of the meal, the letter from Colonel Jameson arrived. I did not see the contents, but Arnold read them with some distress. Then, quite politely, he excused himself, saying he had business to attend to. Even so, he was careful to invite the messenger to eat at his table. I did not know it, but after the briefest interview with his wife, Arnold had fled the place.*
>
> *Hammy and McHenry, Lafayette's aide, arrived shortly after, and they were told that General Arnold had gone over*

to West Point, which we all thought fitting since General Washington had also gone over, having decided to visit there before coming to the house. It should have seemed odd to me that Arnold had not told me and the messenger that he was also going to West Point. And it should have seemed odd to all of us at the house that we heard no salute of cannon for General Washington's visit. Now I understand the things that should have raised my suspicions, but then I had none, so complete was my belief in the man.

When His Excellency arrived at Beverly, suddenly all was discovered, for the rider bearing the confiscated papers caught up with him at last. We had changed our route on our return from Connecticut, so the man had traced old ground until he was set on the proper course. By such a small matter, so much was lost! Everything conspired against us and for Arnold. As soon as His Excellency saw the papers, he knew all. He sent Hammy and McHenry after Arnold, but he had already escaped on his barge to the Vulture, a fitting name for a vessel that would take such carrion aboard. In further treachery, the bargemen he commanded to carry him there were made prisoners of the enemy. And his hapless wife, left behind with their child, the terror of her abandonment was awful to behold. She wept and screamed and begged pitifully, sure that she and her child would be killed. We are all convinced of her innocence in the matter, and of course, the general would never harm woman or child. I begrudge Arnold any word of praise, but he did send a letter immediately from the Vulture protesting his wife's innocence and asking that she be well treated.

No one, not even Mistress Arnold, has suffered a more severe wound from this treason than has His Excellency. That he should be so punished after all his loyalty to the man is intolerable. Never have I seen him so grim with rage and grief. Were Arnold brought to him now, I think he would dispatch him with his own hands.

There is one light in the darkness. We cannot know for a certainty, but it is likely that the British planned to seize

*General Washington as part of this plot, for Arnold knew of
his coming and could easily have told the enemy. At least His
Excellency is still with us.*

*The main fort at West Point was Fort Arnold. The name
was changed forthwith, and Arnold's name will be stricken
everywhere from American honor, but, like Judas, he has
carved it in our souls.*

By the time Addie finished reading the letter to her aunts, her voice
was shaking with her own blend of rage and grief.

"That hell-born bitch! She knew, she knew it all! I will never believe
her ignorance. Her Tory leanings, her enjoyment of the British occupation of Philadelphia, and her friendship with John André—none of
those are secrets, and yet Ad and all the others succumbed to her pose
of distress. Poor fools! I wish I had been there. And Arnold, a Judas
indeed! I wonder how much they paid him, for I am sure they did. I
know enough about André to know he had no need to carry plans of
West Point. With his intelligence and his artist's eye, he could easily
have waited until he was back in New York to commit the plans to
paper. Those were Arnold's plans, something tangible to sell." She
stopped, conscious of how offensive her ranting must be to her aunts,
but both of them were white-faced, fixed on the same point.

"What would we do if the enemy took Washington from us?"
Camille whispered. "He is our lodestar; without him, we are lost."

And Catherine said, "Such a heavy burden for one man to carry.
How he must long to lay it down."

Their mutual strength had fled for the moment. They looked so
frightened, Addie's fury drained away with the realization that everywhere Patriots were staggering from the blow Arnold had dealt them.
Everywhere they were questioning whom they could trust and whether
they could ever prevail against the misfortunes that beat against them.

At Castleton, they were briefly elated by the news that in early October,
a large force of Tories led by a British officer had been destroyed at

King's Mountain in South Carolina at the border with North Carolina. The victory had been so complete, Cornwallis had retreated south from the position he had established in Charlotte, North Carolina.

But then, as more details were revealed, they learned it had been as much a slaughter as a battle, for even when the Tories had been overrun completely and were trying to surrender, the killing went on as the frontiersmen called for "Tarleton's Quarter," which meant no quarter at all. Only the intervention of some of those recognized by the frontiersmen as commanding officers had allowed for survivors.

"Banastre Tarleton is as despicable as reputation has him. He is a cold, cruel man who loathes 'provincials.' But I fear the idea that we must stoop to his depths," Addie said, haunted by the image of battles where the action didn't stop until all the defeated had been put to death by musket or blade, by boot or fire. Her mind was too agile in conjuring the ways to end life, and she realized how ever present Iain was to her because she immediately thought of how little quarter the British troops had given the Highlanders at Culloden. They had not only killed many of the wounded when the battle was over, but they had also, for years after, hunted down those who were loyal to the Stuarts. They had beheaded Iain's father.

Catherine, usually so mild and measured, did not share Addie's moral reservations. "Honor in war cannot work unless both sides agree to the same rules. It is unfortunate the rules are bending and breaking in this war, but I would smash every one of them to keep my sons and nephews alive."

It was difficult to argue ideals against such vital interests, and Addie didn't try.

The most heartening news was that General Greene was traveling south to take command and reorganize what was left of the Southern Department. At long last, the Congress was paying attention to General Washington's wishes. General Greene was one of the best and steadiest of Continental officers and, just as important, Washington trusted him without reservation, even after Arnold's betrayal. Addie spared a thought for Kitty, who would fret at having her husband so far from her, for it was sure that unlike the wives of common soldiers, officers' wives would not be following their husbands to the dangers of the Carolinas.

Christmas at Castleton was much more spartan than in previous years, but it was celebrated nonetheless, with extra food and new clothing, and time away from work for the slaves' own festivities. But the best gift arrived after the holiday when Justin, Hart, and Reeves appeared without prior notice. Lee's legion was being sent to report to Greene for duty, and the three men could spend only a night at Castleton, it being a special privilege that they were allowed to be there at all.

The tall young men in their green-jacketed uniforms and their high boots swept in like a strong wind, charging the atmosphere with the crackling energy of a lightning storm. Word of their coming swept the plantation, Sissy and Rand were sent for, and Catherine and Camille kept wiping tears from their eyes, smiling all the while, both of them more flustered than Addie had ever seen them.

Though separation had not been nearly as long for her as for her aunts, Addie was only slightly calmer than they when she greeted Justin.

He embraced her without hesitation. "You look beautiful! Motherhood becomes you. You could not pass for a boy now," he teased. "When can I meet the miraculous child who has wrought such a transformation?"

When Addie put Johanna into his arms, Justin held the baby gingerly, afraid he might inadvertently harm this small being. He looked into the rosy little face, and blue eyes stared back at him. Then Johanna smiled as if she found Justin wholly delightful, and he fell in love. He could see his sister in the slightly almond shape of the baby's eyes, in myriad details, but the black hair and the eyes he knew would stay blue were Colonel Traverne's. Much clearer than glimpses of him in battle, Justin could see the big Highlander waiting to escort Addie to New York, he could feel the solid presence of the man, the commanding strength. Suddenly the last of his reservations vanished, and he was infinitely grateful that Addie had had Traverne to comfort and love her after Silas died.

There was no more awkwardness; Johanna fit in his arms, her unwavering gaze of fascinated acceptance flowing over him in a warm wave. "Addie, she is blessing enough for all time. There are no enemies here."

Addie tucked her head into the hollow of his neck, putting her arms around him and Johanna, and when she could control her voice, she stepped away so that she could see his face.

"Colonel Traverne and Darius, they continue with Cornwallis, don't they?"

"Yes." It was futile to lie.

"Send me news of them if you have it. But neither of them is to know about Johanna." She could imagine Justin sending word through the lines from some misguided notion of making things right. "Iain offered me marriage, and he worried there might be a child, though I told him there could not be. I will not go to a country ruled by my enemies, and I will not cause him to forsake his country or to compromise his honor or duty for my loyalties."

"But you do love him?"

"Yes, I love him well, and I count myself a most fortunate woman to have found a second chance to love and be loved by a good man. But the war has changed the shape of everything." Her smile was wistful. "It is a puzzle within a puzzle. Because of the war, I cannot marry Iain. But without the war, I would never have met him, and I would not have lost Silas as I did, nor would I have Johanna. I am thankful it is not in my power to change the past, for I would not like to have to make the choice between Silas and my daughter."

Holding his niece in his arms, Justin knew he would not want to make that choice either.

Justin had brought a letter for Addie from her twin, but she was more interested in what Justin had to say about him.

"It must have been difficult for him to see all of you ride away."

Justin nodded. "Yes, especially because you are away from him, too. But he has Matilda, and after this hellish business with Arnold, our brother is even more solicitous of the general than before. He would not leave him now. Has he told you there had been some talk of him going to France as Special Minister to the Court of Versailles, to tell the French of our current plight and of how much more assistance we need?"

Addie's surprise was so evident, Justin went on.

"I didn't think he would note it in his letter. It was a long chance in any case. John Laurens is the one the Congress wants. But now that his exchange is complete and he is no longer a prisoner, he desires nothing so much as to return to the fighting in the Carolinas. At least while he was on parole, he was allowed to meet with his father before Mr. Laurens sailed for Holland to beg a loan for us from the Dutch. Word has come that the ship was taken by the British. John's father is a prisoner in the Tower of London."

Addie gasped in horror, and she didn't have to explain to Justin that she was thinking of Silas.

"Henry Laurens is a prominent man, and he has many important connections in England. It is bad for our cause that so able an advocate can no longer serve us, but the enemy is not going to harm him," he assured her with such confidence, Addie had to believe him.

"John suggested that Hammy or Ad go to France in his place, but Hammy wasn't overly enthusiastic. He married his Betsey a fortnight ago, and there are always whispers about his origins." Justin kept his voice even because he didn't want to disturb the baby, but his jaw was tight with anger. "There has been talk about Ad's heritage, too, because of Papa and Darius. No one but a fool would have any doubts left regarding Ad's loyalty or mine after our long service, but that doesn't change the fact that both Papa and Darius are well-known Loyalists. And some think that would compromise Ad's effectiveness in France. So John will be going despite his reluctance."

"What a tawdry piece of absurdity it is that anyone should question your worth or Ad's!" Addie snapped, but she was angry only for the insult, not because Ad would miss the prestige and adventure of going to France. He was too distant as it was; she didn't want him to risk being taken by the enemy at sea or to be so far away as France.

"It is just as well," she said. "It is an odd pairing, but General Washington and Matilda need Ad to be with them. And no matter how much John wants to dash off to battle again, he is a clever choice for this mission. He was educated in Europe. His father's prominence and current imprisonment must count in his favor to prove how deep loyalty runs in his family. And if he but remembers, he has a wife and child in England. He has never seen his daughter." Her eyes caressed Johanna, and she did not deny to herself how much Iain would want to see her did he know of her existence. "I understand why his wife has not dared the dangerous crossing to the United States, but there must be a way she and their child can join him in France."

Justin laughed, and the deep rumbling sound against her made Johanna kick and crow happily in echo. "Trust you to think of the practical above all the sly twists and turns of politics," he said. But then he sobered. "Because of Arnold, I think General Washington is more isolated and lonely than he has been since the war began, though Mistress Washington is with him. He needs to have Ad, Tench, and others who have been with him for so long to stay beside him now."

By the time they rejoined the others, Sissy and Rand had arrived, and although Rand was shy of the men at first, before long he was shrieking with joy as his uncles and Cousin Justin vied for his attention, swinging him around, giving him pretend horseback rides, and playing any game he chose until, by early evening, he was so exhausted he fell asleep in Hart's arms despite the chatter going on all around him.

"You've got a splendid son," Hart told his sister. "James would be so proud of him."

"I am glad he saw Rand born," Sissy said, but even mention of her dead husband did not lessen her bliss at seeing her brothers again.

She was resolute in keeping her mind off how short the visit would be, and Addie tried to do the same, but she could almost hear the minutes ticking away. She tried to store up every word that Justin said, every expression, and gesture. And the minutes with Hart and Reeves were no less precious, for her cousins cooed over Johanna and praised Addie for producing her as if there were nothing untoward in the baby's existence.

Morning came much too soon.

Addie clung to Justin, and he murmured, "General Greene and all of us, we will do our best, but we may not be able to prevent Cornwallis from reaching Virginia. Don't wait too long. Go north if the enemy threatens."

Even when Castleton was far behind him, Justin could still hear the warning Addie had offered in return for his, the words spoken without a quaver.

"If it comes to a choice between your life and Darius's or Iain's, don't hesitate, not for my sake or for Johanna's. Save your own life. I love them both, but I love you and Ad more."

For the first time, Justin admitted to himself his full disenchantment with the war, but he was resolved that he would see it through until it ended or he did.

Chapter 2

Winter 1781

After Addie had reread Ad's letter and the note in it from Matilda, she burned it. It was one of the hardest of Hartley's instructions to follow, but Addie, her aunts, and Sissy were complying, burning all correspondence that contained any news of the Continental Army or the Congress. That meant nearly every letter they received, and for Addie, with her background in books and printing, it was particular agony to destroy the words that recorded the struggle of her brothers and Matilda to keep faith and believe that victory would come despite all the hardships and losses. Had she a choice, she would have kept the letters for Johanna, for all the children of the next generation, so that they would know what it had been like to fight for independence against such odds, so that they would know, even if freedom had not been won by their time.

There was always a chance a letter would be intercepted by the enemy, but it would be far worse if a large collection of them, with all the information they contained, were discovered at Castleton. The silver and other valuables had been buried, but that did not guarantee they would not be found. However, the enemy could not reclaim words that had vanished in smoke.

They came so soon after Justin, Hart, and Reeves had left, the first news of unusual traffic on the river raised the hope that the wonderful visit was going to be repeated, but hope turned to fear when the lookout came in shouting, "Redcoats! Many, many redcoats!" The young slave's skin was muddy with fear, his eyes wide.

After an initial burst of panic, Catherine, Camille, and Addie moved swiftly. The best of the saddle horses that remained, including Nightingale, were sent into the deep woods, shadowed even in the winter, to the rough enclosure that had been constructed there. Two of the stablemen stayed with them while two others came back, obliterating the prints of the hooves with a sweep of a brush.

Food supplies—meats, salted fish, dried peas, beans, and fruits, milk, butter, and eggs, corn, wheat, and more—were hidden in the thickets, though much was left in place to avoid raising suspicion. The women with small children were, like the horses, sent to shelter in the woods. Addie hated the comparison between livestock and human beings that rose in her mind, but there was no help for it.

A rider carried a warning to Bright Oak and other plantations accessible by road, but aside from these efforts to follow Hartley's instructions and preserve what they could, there was nothing the women could do to halt the invasion.

Her aunts wanted Addie to stay inside with Johanna as the enemy approached the house, and she was considering it when she identified the commanding officer through a spyglass.

"My God! It is General Arnold! Of all the dogs to set upon us." Briefly she contemplated waiting until he was close enough to the house for a musket ball fired from a window to have a chance of hitting his heart or his brain. But then Castleton would be razed to the ground.

"We are truly lost," Catherine said in despair.

"Not if you allow me to approach him. His wife gave a magnificent performance for General Washington, Ad, and others; Arnold deserves the same from me, though I doubt my thespian skills are the equal of Peggy's. But, please, let me try." Addie's rage had overcome her fear, and nothing seemed more important than that she might have the chance to deceive Arnold, the greatest deceiver of them all.

"We have no time to discuss this, and it seems the best course we have." Camille's voice was calm, but her hands were shaking.

They watched the British unloading men and horses from the small fleet of boats coming into the landing, and Addie's heart skipped a beat as she saw the green-coated figures among them. But they were not Darius's men; they were Simcoe's Queen's Rangers. There were other Loyalists and some Hessians with the British regulars too.

It was Addie who stepped forward to greet the party when it approached.

"General Arnold, Colonel Simcoe, welcome to Castleton." She curtseyed as they dismounted, and her glance included other officers she recognized. "These are my aunts, Mistress Castleton and Mistress Stanhope." She silently applauded the two women, for they curtseyed, too, murmured welcome, and smiled softly with all their Virginia charm, as if there was nothing amiss in seeing before them a once-trusted Continental officer now clad in the bright red coat of the enemy.

"Gentlemen, have you news of my brother, Darius Valencourt, or of Colonel Traverne?" This was her weapon; and she allowed her real concern for her brother and Iain to show. "I have had no word of them since I left New York."

Though Arnold had quickly cloaked his surprise at her presence at Castleton, Addie had seen it. He had not known she would be in Virginia. And Simcoe certainly had not; he was regarding her with a mixture of shock, distaste, and unease. There had been no warmth in their encounters in New York, but he was Darius's friend, and Simcoe had witnessed the affection between the siblings.

Thinking of Peggy Arnold fooling General Washington and his aides with her histrionics, Addie raised a hand to her brow. Tears filled her eyes, and her mouth trembled.

"Oh, pray tell me no harm has befallen them! This is all so difficult and awkward, for we are the same people, yet not the same at all because the war divides us. Still, there are ties of affection that cannot be broken. Darius is my brother and Colonel Traverne is my friend. And you, General Arnold, were so important in the recovery of another of my brothers. I do not think my twin would have healed so fully without your kindness. Your visit to us in Philadelphia made him believe he could keep his leg and walk again, and so he has."

She saw it then, the same capitulation to female hysterics that Peggy Arnold had won. Arnold and Simcoe were nonplussed by her behavior, and they responded instinctively to her plea for information and to her deliberate blurring of the line between enemies and friends.

"They remain with General Lord Cornwallis, and I have not heard that any ill has befallen either of them," Simcoe offered gruffly.

"Thank you, Colonel Simcoe. You cannot know what balm this is to my spirit." She turned her attention to Arnold, thinking she could never grow accustomed to seeing the erstwhile hero clad in a British uniform, but her face showed nothing but concern. "Your wife, sir, she is well? Poor lady, this must have been a most trying time for her." Addie felt quite cunning, for without mentioning West Point, she had reminded him of how generously General Washington and his aides had behaved toward Peggy.

"She and our son joined me in New York, and her spirits are recovering, though she was treated most uncivilly in Philadelphia and was forced to leave." His dark eyes sparked with sudden fury.

"But surely it is better that she and your child be with you, where they belong," Addie said. Inwardly she was more shocked by him than before because she realized he was so blind to the evil he had done, he could not comprehend why government officials and those citizens of Philadelphia who were loyal to the United States had demanded that Peggy be banished from their city.

"Addie, we mustn't keep these gentlemen standing outside all day," Catherine's voice chided gently. "Pray, sirs, come into the house that we may offer you refreshment."

Addie's heart pounded as she waited to see what the officers would do. If they accepted the hospitality of the house, it was less likely they would burn it down. Catherine and Camille were playing their parts to perfection, looking rather lost and fluttery, as if attempting to maintain their old standards of hospitality in a world they no longer recognized.

Arnold, Simcoe, and some of their officers followed Catherine and Camille into the house, and with a sigh of relief, Addie joined them, resisting the impulse to look back at the small army on Castleton grounds. The troops were spreading out, inspecting the stables and various other buildings, ostensibly to make sure there were no hidden soldiers waiting to fire on them, but they were also making a careful inventory of livestock and everything else. And the same process went on in the house, with the Castleton women pretending not to notice as booted feet tramped about, though Arnold, Simcoe, and a few other officers stayed with the women, nibbling the food the slaves brought, sipping the wine Catherine poured for them. The men were ill at ease, which Addie judged all the better, as they might leave more quickly. She heard footsteps going upstairs, and she resisted the impulse to race after the men and bar them from Johanna. Her breasts ached, and she hoped her milk wouldn't leak or Johanna begin to howl for her. If the baby were mentioned, she would have no choice but to tell her lie, though Simcoe knew when Silas had died. He might recognize the father in the child, and one way or the other, word would get back to Darius and Iain. And she did not know if Ad had told Arnold of the child during his brief meeting with him at West Point, or if Arnold would remember such news anyway, given how momentous that day had been for him. Her web of deception seemed very fragile.

The footsteps came back down the stairs, but no mention was made of the infant watched over by a Black woman. The soldiers saw no interest or value in the child; they were searching for more useful items.

One of the searchers spoke low to Arnold, who nodded and then addressed the women.

"Were we to look further, would we find more of the wealth—the silver and fine horses—reputed to be here?" He asked it as smoothly as if he were inquiring about the weather.

Catherine answered serenely, as if there were no threat or insult. "You would need to look back in time before the war stripped so much from us, as it has from so many. Why, if you visit again, you may find that even the last of the pewter has been taken from us, melted down for the lead to make musket balls. Like your wife, we are mere women, buffeted by every unkind wind of war's misfortune."

This eloquence was almost too much for Camille, who, with quick effort, turned a snort into a small sob and hid her face in her hands until she had regained control.

The officers' anxiousness to leave grew increasingly evident, and Addie noticed an odd thing: Simcoe gave Arnold a slight nod before Arnold announced, "We must be on our way."

In that unguarded moment, Addie saw in Simcoe contempt for a superior officer, and it occurred to her that Simcoe had been sent as much to chaperone Arnold as to cooperate with him, an indication that General Clinton did not fully trust his new general. She realized that, as Simcoe had been a close friend of Major André, it must be galling to be in the company of the man who bore much of the responsibility for his friend's death. She had noted the black and white feathers decking the bridles of the horses belonging to Simcoe's men, and she suspected they were tokens of mourning for André.

The women said nothing when they saw the soldiers carrying food out of the meat and smoke houses, the springhouse, the dairy, granary, and every other storage space. The food the women had left in place seemed little enough tribute to pay for protecting everything else. And there was nothing they could do about the theft anyway.

But then Addie saw some of the redcoats speaking to the slaves who had gathered in nervous groups to watch the invaders. At first she thought the redcoats might he asking where Castleton's movable wealth had been secreted, but Camille guessed the truth.

"No!" she wailed. "You mustn't take our people! They will be helpless!"

"We will not 'take' them. We will allow those who wish it to come with us. They will not be helpless; they will be free," Arnold corrected smoothly.

"But—" Camille began to protest further.

But Catherine stopped her. "There is nothing we can do. They are using neither force nor threat to make them go."

It was true. There was no sign of overt coercion. Instead, the soldiers were using the most powerful force of all, promising freedom but selecting only those who would be useful and hardy enough to travel with them. In the end, five strong young men went with them. One of them was Hebe's only surviving child, Josiah, who was not yet twenty.

When Hebe saw he was going, she ran to him, clutching at him, trying to drag him back physically, screaming, "No, don't go, lies, all lies, no, Josiah, no!" but it was to no avail.

Josiah firmly detached his mother's grasping arms. "I have to go, but I be back for you when the King make us all free."

Hebe crouched on the ground, hiding her face in her apron, unable to watch her son leave with the others. Catherine and Camille were caught in place, tears trickling down their cheeks, now truly devoid of their normal competence.

Addie went to Hebe. She knelt beside her and put her arms around her. "I am so sorry, Hebe, so very sorry. But maybe he will be freed, maybe—"

Hebe shook her head violently. "No, they lie! They don't care 'bout my boy, they jus' use 'im."

Arnold seemed bored by the scene, but Simcoe appeared uncomfortable with this further display of emotion, and before they rode away, he said, "Mistress Bradwell, I will send word to your brother and Colonel Traverne that you are well and concerned about them."

"Thank you, Colonel," she murmured, though she believed he made the offer more to separate himself from Arnold than to accommodate her.

While the troops moved off overland, the boats proceeded upriver, indicating that perhaps the soldiers would not return here. It was a great blessing on a bleak day.

Everyone stood as motionless as if overtaken by a sudden winter frost until the last of the troops and boats had vanished from sight. Hebe's sobs subsided to faint whimpers. Then slowly, the slaves began to drift back to their work, though many of them continued to cast glances in the direction the enemy had taken.

Catherine assumed the care of Hebe, leading her into the house, speaking to her gently.

"You saved us a great deal of grief," Camille told Addie. "Without you, our losses would have been much, much worse."

"Perhaps not." Addie was suddenly so exhausted, it was an effort to speak. "Perhaps they got what they wanted here, after all. They showed us they are in control and can raid where they will. Perhaps they would have liked the silver and horses; perhaps a fire would have pleased them; but they got five strong men to work for them, and we were not their objective. Castleton was just a minor excursion. It is Richmond they want."

It was hard for her to think of Richmond as the capital, but it had come to her as she had spoken to Arnold and Simcoe that they were following the James River, not for the wealth of the plantations along it, but because it led to the seat of Virginia's government. It was a most exquisite affront to General Washington, to send the traitor Arnold there to prove that Richmond was no more secure than Williamsburg.

"I need to go to Johanna. Please tell me if word comes from Sissy," Addie said, and Camille did not try to detain her.

Even feeding Johanna did not calm the thunder in Addie's heart, and when the baby squirmed and mewed in protest, Addie realized how tightly she was holding her.

"I'm sorry, sweet lamb, no one will hurt you, no one." Her voice trembled with reaction to everything that had happened.

She reminded herself that though five men had gone with the enemy, Castleton still stood. But that did not mitigate the horror of being in Arnold's company. She felt as if she'd been eye to eye with a venomous snake, waiting for it to strike. She put Johanna down and made it just in time to the chamber pot. She continued to retch long after her stomach was empty.

It was a relief to learn that Bright Oak had not been visited by the enemy, but a pall hung over Castleton. The avoidance of Bright Oak suggested that Arnold was indeed anxious to attack Richmond, but more immediate than that threat was the disquiet left in the wake of the men who had joined the enemy. The whispered conversations among those who remained were made more conspicuous because they ceased the instant one of the white women drew near, but Addie did not fear the slaves would harm her or her aunts. Having Josiah and the others leave had upset everyone.

Addie's heart ached for Hebe, and also for Catherine and Camille. Her aunts were furious at the enemy for luring the men away with promises they believed to be false, but beyond that, they were profoundly hurt and confused by what they perceived as the slaves' disloyalty.

"Our people are very well treated. Those who left are going to find life away from Castleton very harsh," Camille said.

Catherine added, "I pity them, for they are children, easily deceived, easily bribed by so little as a bit of bright cloth."

Addie knew it would be better if she refrained from commenting, but she could not.

"I am sure there are many slaves here who, if given the same opportunities as Tullia had, would flourish as she has. And those who left today, they did not go for a 'bit of bright cloth,' nor did they betray us, though they could have curried favor by telling where everything is hidden. They went for the promise of freedom. If they are deluded to risk so much for it, then are we not, too? To be independent of tyranny; to be free to pursue our own lives in our own way; does not the same force that drives them drive us?"

Addie did not see the point in arguing further and Camille changed the subject as if they had not been on dangerous ground and proved that while she might see slavery in the shape she desired, she was clear-sighted about other matters.

"Did you notice that though they ride with Arnold, Colonel Simcoe and the other officers are not pleased to be in his company? It is some little comfort to think that the enemy regards him with scarcely more approval than we do."

"I also saw the dislike," said Addie. "I hope Arnold finds more enemies than friends and is scorned in every quarter. It will not stop the damage he does, but it should diminish his joy in it."

Belatedly, a message arrived from Hartley warning them that Arnold was on his way. They waited through the next tense days for news, feeling isolated and vulnerable, but determined not to flee. Sissy, of the same mind, remained at Bright Oak.

Heavy rain drenched the land, turning the earth to red mud and distorting the air until the enemy could be seen in every dank shadow. In spite of the risks, Camille ordered the horses brought back to their stables, and Catherine had hidden food returned to shelter, both of them deciding that the weather could cause as much damage as the pillaging of the enemy.

The rain had ceased, but there was high mist on the river when the flotilla of boats reappeared, and it was as if breathing at Castleton stopped. But the enemy passed on down the river, while those watching strained and failed to catch a glimpse of Josiah and the others.

They were safe at Castleton, but in Richmond shops, magazines, warehouses, and sundry other properties, excluding those belonging to Loyalists, had been put to the torch when the merchants had refused to relinquish their goods at half value unless Governor Thomas Jefferson approved. But Jefferson and other members of Virginia's government had prudently escaped across the river, and that put an end to any parley.

"His offer to the merchants reveals the man," Addie told her aunts. "I cannot know what he would have done with the goods had his offer been accepted, but as he has proven himself to be a man who views everything with an eye to personal gain, he might have had some scheme in mind. Maybe Colonel Simcoe has been charged with keeping Arnold from defrauding the British Army." She got some satisfaction from speaking so meanly of the man.

The enemy was gone for now, quartered at Portsmouth, but that was not so distant and offered scant solace when coupled with the knowledge that the troops could return whenever they willed with little expectation of opposition. Baron von Steuben, who had been so effective in organizing and training the troops at Valley Forge, had enjoyed no such success since he had been sent to Virginia to organize her defenses. He had few regular troops, and the militia that was left in the state did not respond to his style of command, when they showed up at all. It was no secret that he had rapidly come to regard them as worthless and untrainable.

He had an unlikely ally in Camille, who forsook her usual defense of anything Virginian to say, "The best of our men are up north with General Washington or down south with General Greene. Virginia can have no chance against the enemy until there is an adequate army on her soil, and Lord knows where that could come from."

"If only the French and American forces can find a way to cooperate against General Clinton in New York…" Addie gave up her feeble attempt at encouragement because the truth was that competent action from the joint forces seemed as far away as ever. The French Alliance was proving as disappointing as skeptics had predicted. For an instant, Silas's face was clear to Addie as she remembered his deep reservations about trusting those who had so recently been enemies. Then his image was gone, leaving emptiness and sorrow in its wake.

The news from the north deepened the gloom. The new year had begun with mutiny in the ranks of some of the best of the Continental troops, the Pennsylvania Line, which in turn had emboldened men in the New Jersey Line to take like action. The soldiers had long passed beyond their limits by the lack of pay, food, uniforms, and everything else; they wanted what was owed to them. Though the mutinies were settled by an uneasy mix of negotiations between officers and men, the tragedy was that Washington, a daily witness to the deprivations of his men, had long dreaded just this situation. Men like Hartley had seen the danger, too, but there had not been enough of them to force the Congress to provision the army adequately.

Addie's heart ached for General Washington and for the officers and men who had remained loyal through so much. No blow from the enemy could be as crippling as collapse from within, and defeat seemed more possible than ever before. Washington was chronically short of troops, and if he could not depend on the small number he had, it was only too possible that the war would simply end with the dissolution of the Continental Army. No aid from France or any other power could fill that void.

After so many years of fighting, after such faith and sacrifice, it was intolerable that it should all be in vain. Her brothers, cousins, and uncle would be as vulnerable to arrest, imprisonment, and execution as Washington and his generals. She did not imagine that the King and Parliament would be overly merciful at this late stage after the upstart United States had caused them such trouble and expense.

Addie did not give voice to her depressing thoughts, but she could see her fear in her aunts' faces. It was as if the three of them had an understanding that to speak aloud of defeat might somehow make it more probable. When Sissy came to Castleton, she, too, was part of the silence, determinedly cheerful as if she did not dread the fate of her father and brothers.

Then they received word of an American victory over Tarleton's Legion at a place called Hannah's Cowpens in South Carolina, not far from the border with North Carolina. It was a well-known spot used for wintering cattle and General Daniel Morgan had chosen it for his camp in order that militia units might find him easily. Morgan was severely afflicted with arthritis and had retired to his Virginia farm nearly two years ago, but after the disaster at Camden, he had rejoined the army. The only thing stronger than the pain in his joints was his hatred for the British. He bore the scars of five hundred lashes received during the French and Indian War when he had run afoul of a British officer's bad temper.

It was a stunning victory because Tarleton's Legion had gained a reputation for being invincible. But Morgan had crushed it, killing many and taking more prisoner, and he had done it by perfectly understanding the varying capabilities of his men. He had not asked the various militia companies to stand fast like regular troops, he had instructed them to fire three volleys as their turns came and then to withdraw in orderly retreat while the Continental infantry and cavalry swept the field. This gave the militia the chance to reform, without asking more of them than they were trained to do.

As his legion was being crushed, Tarleton had become enraged, ordering a last attack by his dragoons. They refused the command. Tarleton gathered some men and charged anyway, but it was a futile gesture. American cavalry drove him off, and the British abandoned the field.

It was a sweet victory for Addie. Since coming south with General Clinton for the attack on Charles Town, Tarleton had won wide, if dubious, renown for swift, ruthless attacks on pockets of American resistance in the Carolinas, attacks that had taken many lives in action and many in the aftermath with Tarleton's Quarter accounting again and again for the slaughter of those who tried to surrender. And Tarleton's Legion and Lee's Legion were particular enemies; any lessening of Banastre Tarleton's effectiveness was good for Lee's men. Addie's only regret was that Tarleton had escaped after the battle. Her relief was that Darius had not been with him. Though Tarleton had been a guest at Darius's house, Addie did not think the two men would share the field with any ease. Not only their styles of combat, but also their purposes were different. Darius wanted victory to ensure that he could go on as before, a loyal Englishman prospering in the colonies; Tarleton, with his contempt for all things American, could want nothing so much as to return victorious to England where he could enjoy the fame of his military exploits.

Addie assumed Darius and Iain were still with Cornwallis, but she would have little chance of knowing if they were sent back to New York. There had been only a short message from Justin, Hart, and Reeves since their visit, just an assurance that they had rejoined Harry Lee and were under General Greene's command. And even were Justin privy to the kind of personal news about Darius and Iain that Addie desired, she could not expect him to fill his letters with it.

She had thought she was handling the uncertainty of these days and nights with admirable calm, but her body belied her. Her milk slowed and then stopped altogether so that Johanna had to be wet-nursed by one of the slaves who had an infant younger than Johanna and plenty of milk. Though her aunts assured her that this situation was not unusual, Addie felt inadequate that she could no longer nurse her child, and she missed the pull of the little mouth on her breasts and the power of knowing nourishment was flowing from her to her daughter. In further repudiation of her claim to motherhood, the softer curves she had acquired disappeared, leaving her nearly as angular as she had been when she had dressed as a boy.

Addie knew she was behaving irrationally, but she became obsessed with Johanna's wellbeing, fearful that every shift in the baby's mood heralded the onset of some terrible illness, and a process as natural as teething made her fuss more than her daughter. She understood as never before why some parents were determined not to risk too much affection for a child during the first year or so when so many died, but that aloofness was denied her; she had loved Johanna long before the baby had been born and had taken her first breath.

Finally, when Addie's fretting over the baby had reached the point of adding to everyone's anxiety, Camille took her in hand.

"I do not have children of my own, though I've helped to raise a few. But I do have common sense, while you seem to be losing yours. Johanna is a healthy, happy little girl except when her mother is frightening her. Addie, Johanna is not the war nor even the smallest skirmish in it. You are making her into a field of battle, though the enemy is not in sight." Camille spoke the harsh words so gently, the sting was blunted, and her voice softened further when she asked, "Do you believe you have made some bargain with Providence that if you keep Johanna from harm, you will also keep safe everyone else you love, everyone you love on both sides of the conflict? It doesn't work that way, my dear, and give thanks that it does not, else we would all be forced to terrible bargains—this life for that one, a child for a brother, a brother for a lover, one friend for another. If these were our decisions to make, we would all be mad. We may be anyway, but it is not because we control what life brings or takes away from us and those we love."

Addie's first impulse was to deny what her aunt had seen in her, but then she saw herself as she had been these past days. It was all true. Somewhere deep inside she had become convinced that if she could protect Johanna, she could protect them all—Justin, Ad and Matilda, Darius, Iain, her cousins, and beyond even to Washington and his officers and men.

The absurdity of it struck her so powerfully, her voice was choked when she agreed, "Madness is the proper word for it."

Camille's smile was wry. "You are not alone. Every time I work in the gardens, I feel as if I am bringing order to the entire world."

When Addie received a letter from Ad in early March, she gave it to Camille, telling her, "It seems my brother needs your counsel as much as I did. He is suffering from that same affliction of feeling responsible for events beyond his control."

She did not blame Ad for his dejection, for Hammy was leaving Washington's staff.

It was such a minor contretemps, it should have caused no lasting harm, but too much pride was involved. Hammy was bearing a letter for the Commissary to Tench when he and the general met on the stairs. The General told Hammy he wished to speak to him, and Hammy replied that he would wait upon him immediately. But on his way back from delivering the letter to Tench, Hammy was waylaid by Lafayette on a matter of business, and the two held a brief conversation before the marquis, an innocent in the action, went on his way. It was a fatal delay, for the general met Hammy at the head of the stairs, and in a high temper, he accused him of showing disrespect by keeping him waiting. "I am not conscious of it, sir, but since you have thought it necessary to tell me so, we part," Hammy said, and the general replied, "Very well, sir, if it be your choice."

The voices carrying too well, Tench and I were unwilling witnesses to the whole sorry affair and yet were incapable of changing the outcome. The general's great flash of temper, though rare, was not unfamiliar to us. He is a man so sorely pressed by duty, the infrequency of these outbursts is more marvelous than that they do happen on occasion. Within the hour, the general had sent Hammy a handsome apology, but even after that and after an interview with the general, Hammy refused to change his mind. Tench and I have been unsuccessful in our attempts to sway him from his purpose. We must be grateful that he has agreed to stay on for some weeks to assist with the great press of work and the meetings with the French, but under the appearance of normalcy, all is disrupted. It is no help that John is finally on his way to France while there is so much to do here.

Tench is always the kindest of souls and insists the quarrel would never have occurred had our war efforts been going more smoothly. But I have darker thoughts. I think Hammy has always regretted leaving the artillery. I think he has never loved the general as the rest of us do and is anxious now to be quit of this often tedious duty in order that he might seek fortune and renown outside of the army, just as he gained a wellborn wife.

Camille understood the import of the letter as well as Addie did.

"Ad must be very fond of Colonel Hamilton to harbor such rancor against him now."

"He is," Addie said. "He found him somewhat difficult to like at first, but he and the other aides have come to value him greatly, not solely for his intelligence and efficiency, but as a friend, too. This defection must seem like another breach of trust, though no treason is involved. So few of the aides have been with General Washington as long as Ad, Tench, and Colonel Harrison, and Hammy not as long as any of those, but he quickly proved his worth. It will be hard for the others to manage without him. There are new officers coming and going from the staff all of the time, but they do not share the same bond as those who have been so long together."

There were other bits of news in the letter, but Ad finished with:

> *I pray the devil Arnold and his kind come no more to Castleton.*
> *I long to see you and Justin and to meet Johanna. Only Matilda*
> *makes it tolerable to be so far from my sister and my brother.*

Addie could feel his pain as if it were hers. Despite the victory at Cowpens, he felt, as she did, that their great effort was falling apart, and if it should come to that, she wanted them to be together. But she was pinned by responsibility, for though the enemy had invaded here, Castleton still seemed a relatively safe place for Johanna until the child was a little older. Addie promised herself that if the struggle were still going on when it was time for the army to go into winter quarters at the end of the year, she would take Johanna and rejoin Ad and Matilda and trust there would be little curiosity about Johanna's paternity.

The one thing for which they could all be thankful was that the paralyzing cold and blizzards of the previous winter had not been repeated in this one, and everywhere spring was coming earlier on the land. At Castleton, this meant the pace quickened to meet the demands of the growing season. The pulse of life awakening and renewing itself was audible music, and once again Addie welcomed every note, marveling that last year Johanna had been inside of her, unseen, but now every day confirmed her individuality and place in the world.

However, Addie could not ignore what the changing seasons would bring to the army. To the north, with Washington, the troops would wait until the spring storms had ceased and the roads had dried and hardened enough to support the traffic of an army on the move. But to the south, General Greene continued to try to accomplish all he could before the oppressive heat of summer became an enemy as dangerous as the British.

Of necessity, with his limited number of troops and the chronic shortage of supplies, Greene was playing the same game with Cornwallis that Washington had long played with the enemy in the Jerseys, Pennsylvania, and New York. He battled only on ground of his choosing, avoiding confrontations where the enemy would have clear superiority, drawing the enemy into long, wearying chases across the rain-swept land.

After Cowpens, Morgan had retreated northward, and Cornwallis had come after him, avid to catch him. It was to no avail, for Morgan pushed hard enough to keep a day's march between them. Even when Morgan joined General Greene, and with the advice of his officers, he resisted the temptation to stand and fight before his men were ready.

The short account Addie received from Justin was afire with his old enthusiasm, though it concerned the northward retreat.

> *It was a grand race! We crossed the Dan just ahead of Cornwallis, so close his dragoons and we had almost become friends, they riding ahead of their army, we protecting the rear of ours, all of us within call of each other. But what a shout was raised when our army realized that General Greene and the rest of us were safely across into Virginia. The river is swollen from the rains, and we had the boats. Cornwallis has none and could not follow. And now we will go back after him before he can raise too many Loyalists to his standard. He fancies he leads the hounds and that we are the foxes, but he's got it quite wrong.*

*We are the hunters, careful and clever, and we will run him
to ground.*

*My only regret is that there is no time for a visit to Castleton.
Kiss the Lady Johanna for me.*

Though Justin had written the letter in February, it had traveled by
a circuitous route, and Addie didn't receive it until mid-March, when
it arrived along with rumors that a big battle had just taken place at
Guilford Court House in North Carolina, not far from the Virginia
border. There followed tense days, for the early reports gave the victory
to the British. But then, more details filtered in, making it plain that
though Cornwallis might claim the prize for being in possession of
the field at the end of the fight, if he continued to pay so dearly for
so little, he would soon have no army left.

Due to his ill health, Morgan had retired again, but General Greene
had learned from Morgan's actions at Cowpens and used the militia
in careful combination with his cavalry and regulars, his force having
grown with recent reinforcements. Toward the end, as the battle swung
back and forth, Cornwallis ordered his artillery to fire grapeshot into
the tangle of both armies, with the result that he killed as many of
his own as Americans. But his desperate action did stop an American
counterattack, and that, plus a gap in the American line, persuaded
General Greene to order a retreat, leaving his fieldpieces behind. The
British pursuit was brief and spiritless, for they had lost nearly twice
as many as had the Americans, the best estimate being that Cornwallis
paid for the day with more than a quarter of his troops.

"This will not please the government nor the citizens of Britain,"
Camille observed. "Though it is infrequently, I do still hear from
friends there. They are growing ever more impatient with this war,
and victories at such a toll will win little praise."

Addie wished she could share her aunt's satisfaction, but while word
came swiftly from Hart and Reeves that they were unhurt, though
disgruntled because an encounter with Hessians had kept them from
the heart of the conflict, there was nothing from Justin. She knew
her cousins would have let those at Castleton know had Justin been

wounded, but the war had taught her that there were blows that did not show on the flesh. When his letter finally did come, she understood that it was her wounds, not his, that concerned him.

After assurances that he was uninjured, Justin addressed the subject that had made him reluctant to communicate at all.

> *Valencourt's Rangers were not part of it. They must be on detached duty, and I am thankful for it. Alas, Colonel Traverne and his men were there, and the Highlanders fought hard and were hard hit. I have debated telling you the truth and have decided you deserve no less. I was not there, but by the best witnesses, Colonel Traverne was wounded, as were many of his men. Many of them died, but not, by all I know, Traverne. If I hear more, you will know it. Meanwhile, believe that he lives. It is strange that I should care for his health nearly as much as you do, but his legacy is so visible in Johanna, I would that she have a living father, though he may be far away in Scotland. You and I and Ad may never see our father again, but that does not diminish the inheritance we have for being part of him.*

For a wild instant, Addie thought of going through enemy lines, of forsaking her careful role of Continental officer's wife and of making herself an outcast among her own people by throwing in her lot with Iain. For that instant, she understood the depth of her love for him that any sacrifice seemed worth it could she go to his aid, could she keep him from dying as Silas had died. Then the reality of her life swept over her. She was no longer sovereign and able to take any gamble she chose. Johanna's needs must be considered above all else. But if Addie could not go to Iain, he was seldom absent from her thoughts, and his men were there, too—Angus, Duncan, and the others. She wondered who had been lost, and she wanted the war to end.

On March 1, the Articles of Confederation had at last been ratified after years of bickering about the disposition of eastern lands and everything else. The articles established the principle of a national government in the realms of making war or peace and fixing state quotas of men and money for the Continental Army, but they did not grant to that national government the right to levy taxes or to raise its own troops. To Addie, the ratification was simply another cause for frustration when the army's need for men and money was so overwhelming.

Addie's gloom deepened when she ceased to hear from Justin. "Light Horse" Harry Lee was a name widely known now, so closely was Harry identified with the light cavalry he commanded, and because of the ability of Lee's Legion to move so swiftly, Greene had detached it from his main body of troops, sending it to cooperate with the militia partisans in attacks on British outposts in South Carolina. Before leaving Greene's camp, Justin and the cousins had sent word to Castleton that communication would be vastly more difficult than before and so not to worry at a lack of it.

Catherine echoed Addie's sentiments when she sniffed, "As if that is any reassurance at all!"

"At least they are well mounted," Camille said, and they all took some comfort and much pride in that.

Harry Lee's men rode big, strong horses bred and raised in Virginia and Pennsylvania; while the enemy, having lost most of their good stock on their journey to the Carolinas, had to make do with the smaller animals of that region. At Guilford Court House, not even Tarleton's hunger for revenge for the beating his legion had taken at Cowpens could compensate for the inferiority of his horses, and he had been unable to turn the tide against the Continental dragoons.

Addie wanted her brother and cousins to have every possible advantage, for Tarleton and his commanding officer had earned nicknames, too. Cornwallis was being called "The Terror of the South" for his unceasing predation on citizens' properties in order to supply his army and to bring the Americans to heel, but Tarleton was "The Butcher" for the dead he left in his wake.

For the time being, both Tarleton's Legion and Valencourt's Rangers seemed to be with Cornwallis, though accurate information was hard to obtain. Addie hoped it was true, for after Guilford Court House, Cornwallis had found it increasingly difficult to supply his men from the land, despite his plundering, and had moved his troops to the port of Wilmington, North Carolina, that he might be supplied by sea. He had left an estimated eight thousand men behind in South Carolina and Georgia to deal with Greene's army, including Lee's Legion. That was bad enough, but not, to Addie's mind, as bad as if Tarleton and Darius were going after Harry Lee and his men. In Virginia, it was Simcoe's troops who were doing much of the raiding, seeking Continental munitions and supplies, confiscating what they wanted from civilian sources, and burning what they could not carry off.

The inhabitants of Castleton lived in a state of siege. Ordinary cycles of the year went on because the land and the livestock demanded it be so, but every vessel on the river and every movement in the brush was a potential threat. And no one forgot that Hebe's son Josiah and the others had gone on to an uncertain fate. That Mount Vernon had suffered similarly to Castleton intensified their feelings of vulnerability; not even General Washington's home was safe. It was as if air to breathe were decreasing by the day.

Visitors became a rarity, for traveling meant risking an encounter with the enemy, and few wanted to leave their property, though Cordelia defiantly continued her sporadic visits. Even Sissy appeared much less frequently, for those at Bright Oak depended on her more than ever now. Needing her cousin's company, Addie went to Bright Oak as often as she could. She was impressed by Sissy's calm strength, so much like Catherine's, and that made it more startling when the mask slipped.

It was proving a wet spring, but this late April day was fair and soft, the sunlight revealing how the green of new growth had overtaken the earth. Leaving Johanna with her aunts, Addie rode to Bright Oak for a visit. Rand greeted her with his usual exuberant, "Cousin Azzie!" but Sissy was subdued. As they walked in the gardens, Rand darted ahead, his progress erratic because he stopped to inspect whatever interested him.

"I do not want to leave Bright Oak or Castleton," Sissy said. "But the war is coming here, closer every day, and there is little to stop the enemy. Where will we go if the war is lost? To France, or Spain, or

Holland? Those countries are our allies in war, and I suppose they will not turn us away if we seek refuge in defeat. But I am not French, Spanish, or Dutch, I am a Virginian and an American, and I want to grow old and die here."

Though Sissy had not raised her voice much above a whisper, Addie heard the words as if she were screaming. Of all the dread possibilities, she had not really faced the practicality of exile.

"But why would we?" She was aware of the stupidity of the question before she had fully framed it.

Sissy answered bluntly, "Some will be able to stay, but we will not, not with Papa's prominence in the Congress, and not with our brothers' conspicuous service in the army. I do not believe that even your Loyalist connections would outweigh Ad's long service with General Washington and Justin's with Harry Lee."

"No, they would not," Addie agreed dully, "and I would not wish it in any case."

Too much had been ventured, too much paid in forfeit. If the war were lost, perhaps the old ties to England could be reshaped, after generations had passed, into some new, more equitable form than that of vassals to a king, but Addie could not imagine living under British rule again, not even to be with her father or Darius or Iain—no, not even for Iain.

Sudden anger swept her, anger at herself and Sissy. "If we cannot keep faith, then how can we expect it of our brothers? We have not surrendered; Virginia is not yet completely under enemy rule; and I will not look to Europe until the redcoats have taken every state from north to south."

Rand chose that moment to run up to them, holding his hand out to display his latest treasures, two delicate, pale-blue, and empty shards of a bird's egg.

"See, the bird done fly away," he announced, utterly confident that only good had come to the tiny creature that had lived inside. "See, Cousin Azzie?" He put the pieces in her hand, a special gift for the visitor. Then he peered more closely at the two women, and the joy in his face was replaced by worry. "I do sumpin' wrong?"

Sissy swept him up in her arms as if he weighed nothing and whirled around with him. "No, you did absolutely right! We were feeling a little sad, but you've made us very happy." She gave him a smacking kiss that made him squirm and giggle before she set him down again. "Go find other treasures to show us." He was out of earshot when she added, "To show us that fragile broken things do not always signify the end but may be just the beginning." She brushed her tears impatiently. "If my son can believe that a fledgling he has not seen exists and has grown enough to fly free, I shall believe it, too."

Addie handed one of the shell pieces to Sissy and carefully wrapped the other in her own handkerchief. "To remind us," she said.

When she had returned to Castleton, she put the shell with Paul Byrne's ring, a keepsake from her time in Boston during the siege. Small disparate tokens of the long war.

Chapter 3

Spring 1781

By May, the most ominous development was that Cornwallis was marching northward to Virginia from Wilmington, North Carolina. Clinton had sent reinforcements under Major General William Phillips into Virginia to supersede Arnold in command and, in addition, Cornwallis's army was further enlarged by three more regiments transferred from New York. With these, the enemy had more than seven thousand men in Virginia, and Tarleton was among them, able to take his legion on swift maneuvers with Simcoe's men. Lafayette's American troops numbered fewer than a thousand, and so it became even more imperative that he dance away from full confrontations with the enemy; skirmishing with Tarleton and Simcoe was dangerous enough.

At Castleton, they saw troops on the river quite often, and it was no longer possible to deny that the enemy had taken control of the state. Though Catherine and Camille continued to believe that Castleton was being spared serious damage because of Addie's relationship to Darius and to Colonel Traverne, they did not allow that belief to influence their ideas about her welfare.

"We have discussed it," Catherine told her, "and we are quite sure we can arrange for you and Johanna to leave Virginia safely. Hartley would welcome you in Philadelphia."

"Thank you, but no. When I leave Virginia, it will be to travel with General Washington's army again, and I am not yet ready to subject Johanna to such conditions." She hid her smile at her aunts' reactions, for though it was clear they were glad she was not leaving, they also seemed surprised—and not completely approving—that she planned to follow the drum again.

It was difficult to retain any optimism when, by the middle of June, Cornwallis was in Richmond and seemed able to move his troops wherever he wished. But despite these reversals, all was not yet lost. In South Carolina and into Georgia, Lee's Legion and the partisans were overcoming one enemy outpost after another, and the enemy continued to withdraw more and more troops toward Charles Town. It was a promising development, evidence that Cornwallis's strength was much less than it seemed. It was one thing if he controlled Georgia, the Carolinas, and Virginia, but it was quite another if his strength south of Virginia was fading, isolating his army from supply lines.

As Camille had predicted, the land itself was punishing the enemy. When General Phillips's troops had joined Cornwallis in late May, Phillips himself had been dead a week of fever, and Cornwallis's troops were also suffering the effects of campaigning in the Carolinas, finding no relief in Virginia's summer as they succumbed to fevers, snake bites, and spreading sores caused by insects. Nor did they find the land generous in yielding enough food for so huge a mass of men and beasts. The Americans suffered, too, particularly those not native to the South, but overall, they were more seasoned to the country and to hardship, and they were not suffocated in heavy wool uniforms, being more likely to feel the results of exposure because of having too little clothing rather than too much. Many of the troops who were fully clothed wore breeches and long, loose-fitting cloth shirts decorated with fringe in the style of the buckskin shirts of the frontier. Though devoid of formality, this garb was so practical, General Washington had long since approved it, and more than one correctly uniformed Continental officer envied the comfort of the looser clothing.

Addie thought of Iain and his men and wondered how the closely woven wool of their tartan served them in the heat. She had given up trying to keep Iain out of her mind; he was there constantly. With Cornwallis's arrival in Virginia had come reports that Traverne's Highlanders were with him and that the regiment was still commanded by Colonel Traverne, though he was not fully recovered from the wounds he had received at Guilford Court House.

Addie acknowledged the treachery of the idea, but she would almost have welcomed Cornwallis at Castleton if Iain were with him so that she could see with her own eyes how Iain fared. But it was not he who stole up the river to the plantation.

Justin and Hart arrived in the pre-dawn light, ferried in a small craft managed by two boatmen. It was a good thing Justin and Hart had had such skilled and loyal help to slip past enemy craft, because neither of them was fit to make the journey on his own. Justin was stuporous with fever; Hart had his right arm in a sling; and both of them were filthy and so thin, to Addie they looked like the prisoners in New York.

Justin had to be carried into the house, but Hart insisted on walking, complaining, "Harry Lee sent us home, told us not to come back until we were healthy enough to be of use to him. Damnation! We could've gotten well with the legion just the same as here." His mother uttered no reproof, but Hart checked himself. "Your pardon, Mama, but it was hard to leave Reeves and the others."

"Harry Lee showed remarkable sense." Catherine's voice was calm, but her eyes were bright with unshed tears.

Justin appeared so ill, Addie's old nightmare began to swirl around her, and though awake, she saw the vast grave swallowing another person she loved. The bizarreness of the vision was not improved by the fact that she and her aunts were still attired in their nightclothes, and in the gray first light, everyone looked ghostly.

Camille patted Addie's cheek sharply. "None of that! We are not going to bury them. We are going to bathe and feed them, and then, God help us, we are going to send them back to Harry Lee. Perhaps you lack it in Boston, but here we have long experience with fevers."

The certainty in Camille's voice pierced the haze surrounding Addie, and she went to work with her aunts and the servants to tend to the men. Hart's wound was a severe cut to his upper right arm, but in spite of the grime that covered the rest of him, he had managed to keep it fairly clean, and there was no sign of putrefaction. He was right-handed and worried that his hand was nearly useless, lacking both strength and coordination, but his mother assured him that because he could move his fingers, the condition was only temporary.

But Addie struggled to cling to her aunts' conviction that Justin's outlook was as good as Hart's. Even after Justin had been bathed, put to bed, and dosed with Catherine's potions and broth, he still looked like some starved forest creature. His face, neck, forearms, and hands were dark from the sun, but the color could not be mistaken for health because he was so thin, his bones poked against his skin. Heat radiated from him, hotter than the warming morning.

She sat with him throughout the day, feeding him liquids, caring for him as if he were Johanna. Sometimes he mumbled, and when she heard Darius's name, she was filled with as much frustration as dread because she could not understand what Justin was saying about him.

The day seemed to stretch forever, but finally it ended with a cool breeze coming in from the river, and Addie thought Justin felt cooler, too, though she wasn't sure. She had bathed his hot skin for so long, she doubted she could judge any changes accurately.

His eyes opened, blazing gold, alert and focused, and his voice was low but intelligible. "Poor Addie, don't look so frightened. I'm not dying. I'm just proving that my Massachusetts blood is too sluggish for the fires of the South." He closed his eyes, opening them again when she urged him to sip some of the broth. He took it so eagerly, she had to caution him against choking.

"I never thought anything so simple could taste so good! But I've never lived on half-cooked potatoes, rice, frogs, and other swamp creatures before." He grinned at Addie's grimace of revulsion. "Actually, with the spice of hunger, you would be amazed at what can be swallowed."

He finished the broth, fell asleep, dozed for a while, and then picked up the conversation as if there had been no pause, speaking of the partisan leaders Lee's Legion had been with over the past weeks.

"Pickens and Sumter are good fighters, though Sumter is too independent and does not always cooperate when we need him. But Francis Marion is an exceptional man. He is small and leathery, but his spirit is vast," Justin said. "In his way, he is as disciplined and dedicated as General Washington, though there is naught of the sporting gentleman about him. He drinks nothing stronger than vinegar and water, and his men are held to a code of honor that allows no abuse of civilians and insists on fair treatment of prisoners taken in battle. 'Swamp Fox' is an apt name for him. He and his band know the swamps as you and I know the streets of Boston. They slip in and out as if they were following roads visible only to them. Addie, it is such a strange world! Dark, dank, with moss hanging from the trees and creatures small and large stirring in the shadows, and then suddenly there will be an island of drier land with grass and flowers and a few big trees for shade, a patch of paradise in the middle of all the mud and rot."

He looked away from her, and Addie thought he was falling asleep again, but he was gathering energy to go on.

She forestalled him, saying, "We can talk later."

But he shook his head restlessly. "No, I want to tell you now. General Marion and his men act honorably toward friend and foe alike, but this is becoming rare, at least where more militia than regulars on both sides are involved. They hate each other with unrelenting fury, and British rule has been so harsh in the region, many Patriots would take vengeance on every Loyalist, man or woman, and their children, too, though before the war, many were neighbors and friends. It is far, far worse than I've seen anywhere else. I cannot imagine the two sides will ever share the land in harmony again."

He drew a deep breath to steady his nerve. "Fort Grierson in Georgia was held by Loyalists. We went against it with Brigadier General Pickens and Georgian militia, and the fort surrendered. Then the screaming started, screams for mercy. Harry Lee, Pickens, and the rest of us did our best, but most of the garrison was slaughtered." For an instant, he put his hands over his ears, still hearing the sounds.

"Addie, Darius is all right, but he was there, on detached duty with his rangers to support the Georgia Loyalists. I got to him in time, but many of his men were killed. I made certain that Darius and those of his men who survived were sent to General Greene as prisoners, so that the militia could not finish their work."

Shivers of horror tunneled up and down Addie's spine, and she took one of Justin's hands, cradling it against her cheek.

"Thank you, thank you for saving his life."

"He means much to me also." He closed his eyes, pretending to sleep because he did not want to weep in front of his sister, but the tears burned behind his eyelids.

The brutality of the scene would never leave him. Forever he would see men being bayoneted, hacked with hatchets, gutted with knives, shot with muskets while they pled for their lives. Their hands, running scarlet with blood, thrown up for protection; eyes rolling with animal fear as realization came to them; the stench of gore, fear, urine, feces, and gunpowder—in those minutes that had seemed an eternity, Justin had seen all the devils in hell. Knowing Valencourt's Rangers were there, he had searched frantically for Darius. He had found him battling for his life, and Justin had gone mad, bellowing at the top of his lungs and slashing with his saber to reach him. He knew he had killed at least one militiaman, and Hart had been right beside him, both of them slashing at their own. Hart's wound had been inflicted by a Patriot.

Despite all the fighting both of them had seen, Justin knew that that day had been different for him and Darius. It was not the first time in the war that surrendering men had been killed, but it was the first time they had witnessed it, and the force of the hatred that had caused the violence had destroyed any last thoughts they had had of a shared peace in the future. They had had little time together, but they had been as close as ever in their lives, brothers and equals, not enemies. Darius was grieved over the loss of so many of his troop, including close friends, and Justin felt his sorrow as if it were his own.

And while Darius wanted news of Addie and Ad, Justin craved any word of their father, and every word spoken was valuable because neither of them could imagine they would have a chance to be together like this again.

They did not speculate about which side would be victorious, but Justin heard the echo of his own heart when Darius said, "I want the war over before it steals more from all of us than we could ever win."

They embraced, and then Darius was led away with the other prisoners, and Justin went on to the attack on nearby Fort Cornwallis, which was held by regulars and took some days to conquer. Forts Grierson and Cornwallis had been protecting Augusta, and with their fall, that town was back in American possession. But Justin felt little elation. He had been fighting his own battle with fever since the legion had raced from South Carolina to Georgia, and he was losing. However, he would have gone on for as long as he could stay in the saddle had not Harry Lee sent him and Hart to Castleton, claiming that the two of them were more liability than help. There was truth in that, for a vital factor in the legion's effectiveness was its ability to move swiftly from one place to another, which required that both men and horses be fit. But Harry did not have to send the two so far to recuperate. He had done it out of rough affection, knowing the care and solace to be gotten at Castleton would make it worth the long trip.

With a twinge of guilt, Justin wondered if Harry Lee had seen that more than his body was afflicted, that the example of Tarleton's Quarter at Fort Grierson had sickened his soul.

Justin admired Harry Lee as a commander and loved him as a friend, but he did not mistake the differences between Harry and himself. Harry had a streak of ruthlessness that fascinated Justin, for while it seemed necessary to a true warrior, it was no less appalling for that. More than once during the campaigns in the Jerseys and New York, Harry had gotten into trouble with equal and superior officers for his insistence on doing things as he wished. He had absolute confidence in his abilities as a soldier, and he could be harsh in his determination to shape the action his way. Two years ago, as he and his men had been scouting Stony Point for General Wayne, Harry had become so obsessed with the need for secrecy that when deserters had been caught, he had not only had one of them hanged on the spot, but had then had the corpse beheaded and the head sent to headquarters to be displayed on a pike as a warning to any who might plan on going over to the enemy with information. To this day Harry Lee could not understand why General Washington had been angry at the beheading, and Justin acknowledged his own cowardice that he had never had the courage to tell Harry that he shared the general's revulsion.

Justin felt he could not talk to Addie about his growing weariness with his life in Lee's Legion; her burdens were heavy enough. And no matter how close to the war she had been from the beginning, she was not a soldier. His longing to see Ad was a sharp pain, but his brother seemed as distant as the moon, and the letters they exchanged irregularly were no substitute for being face to face.

The one thing he knew for sure was that he must return to active duty as soon as possible. This was no time for a faltering spirit or body to thin the ranks. And within a few days of his arrival at Castleton, food, medicine, rest, and care were making a palpable difference. The spells of fever and weakness diminished, and he was able to stay alert for much longer periods. He was charmed by a visit from Sissy and Rand, and enthralled by how much Johanna had grown and how beautiful she was. And, inevitably, though they tried not to worry him, he became aware of how much like a siege it was for those at Castleton and Bright Oak to have the enemy so dominant in Virginia, especially when, near the end of June, Cornwallis moved his troops to Williamsburg. That he should occupy the gracious town that had once been the capital seemed even more of an insult than his destructive visit to Richmond.

Nonetheless, there was cause for hope, and Justin wanted Addie to believe it.

"This is what Harry Lee and others who can see further than I have long desired, that Cornwallis would make himself vulnerable by dividing his army. With so many outposts and forts lost to them, most of those he left behind in the Carolinas and Georgia are drawing in toward Charles Town and Savannah. Cornwallis has lost his supply lines and is finding it difficult to provide for the troops with him. He meant to take Virginia and march on north; instead, he is prowling about looking for a safe haven while Lafayette and Wayne harass him."

"But he can be supplied from New York," Addie protested, though he was saying exactly what she had been telling herself to keep despair at bay.

"Only if General Clinton is willing to weaken his own position by sending more ships and troops to Cornwallis. And Clinton has

General Washington watching him, waiting for the chance to attack. More, whether they arrive or not, Clinton must worry that French ships are on the seas, sailing to aid us. You were in New York and met the man, so perhaps you can judge better than I. Do you think he will risk his garrison to help Cornwallis?"

As Addie thought about it, Johanna crawled across the bed to stare at her uncle and pat his face, babbling happily—an incongruous performance amid the talk of war.

The months in New York came back to Addie so vividly, it was as if she were there again, there with Silas, Darius, and Iain; and she considered what she had learned of Clinton and other high officers of the British Army.

"No, Sir Henry will never hazard his position to help Cornwallis. He is as jealous of him as he is fearful of being bested by General Washington."

The emphatic conviction in her mother's voice caused Johanna to peer at her anxiously. Addie smiled at her and touched her cheek.

"Don't worry, my lamb, nothing is wrong." Her eyes met her brother's. "Uncle Justin is telling me good things."

Justin had seen the shadows in her eyes when she remembered her days in New York and, more, he saw Colonel Traverne every time he looked at Johanna. To his surprise, it made no difference in his affection for the child, and because Addie had not hounded him to discuss the man, he felt more obligated to do so.

"You know that Colonel Traverne is with Cornwallis?" he asked abruptly, and at her nod, he continued. "Darius had little news of him, but enough to know that he seems to be recovering from the wounds he received at Guilford. He got a musket ball in the chest and a saber cut to his face and neck."

He saw the color drain out of Addie's face but went on. "Though Darius did not know about Johanna, and I did not tell him, he is aware that you and Colonel Traverne became good friends in New York." Justin said the words evenly. "And he knew you had asked Colonel Simcoe for news of both of them."

He shuddered inwardly at the image of Simcoe and Arnold invading Castleton, but had to concede that Addie's time in New York had surely been to Castleton's advantage.

He forced himself to tell her the rest. "Darius thought you would want to know that a man named Angus was among those killed at Guilford Court House. He died saving his colonel's life."

Not wanting to distress Johanna, Addie opened her eyes wide to keep her tears from overflowing. "Aonghus Mor, liege man to Iain dubh laidir," she said softly. "Big Angus, liege man to Black John the Strong. One of the women who had a few words of English taught me the names. Even now, many Highlanders have little use for surnames. They know each other better than that. Big Angus, that suited him, not only for the size of his body, but for his heart, too." She brushed at tears that tried to escape. "It was Angus who escorted me back from New York, and he had watched over Iain since Iain was a boy. Iain will be very sad to have lost him."

There was so much love and sorrow in her face, Justin looked away, distracting himself by playing with the baby, and he and his sister did not discuss Colonel Traverne again while Justin was at Castleton.

Each day brought visible improvement in Justin's health and in Hart's as well, for he was regaining use of his hand, exercising his fingers with great concentration. It was dangerous for them to be there, isolated from the protection of their or Lafayette's troops, but Addie dreaded their leaving. She consciously stored memories of being with them, and so did Sissy, who spent as much time as she could at Castleton.

Thus neither of them were as pleased as usual when Cordelia came to visit, because that meant they had to share their brothers. Addie momentarily entertained the unkind suspicion that Cordelia had somehow gotten word of the men's presence, but she could see that the woman's surprise was genuine, and Cordelia suggested that she could leave the next day and return at a better time.

"Ah, but it wouldn't be better for us," Hart protested gallantly, sweeping her a bow.

Justin, who had spent only two days out of bed, suddenly looked much stronger and added his welcome. "The women farther south have every reason to be jealous of the beauty in Virginia. No medicine could be more beneficial than your company."

Addie rolled her eyes at Sissy, who made a little pout of disgust, both of them feeling as if they were mere girls again and hopelessly lacking in the company of a worldly woman. But they couldn't cling long to their jealousy, for Cordelia made every effort to include them; it was their brothers who were acting the fools, trying to outrun each other in their race to win her favor.

"I think she's got her eye on Justin," Sissy whispered.

"I hope so," Addie said. "He looks foolish and happy, and I've just realized that he hasn't looked that way since he was courting Sarah, a lifetime ago, before the war made all of us old. If Cordelia can make him young again, she will have my gratitude."

"You make me wish she would choose Hart, but I think they have known each other too well for too long. Hart was ever careful to stay out of her coils, though I reckon he regrets that now."

Addie thought of all Cordelia had lost, not only her husband and stepchildren, but also her child, and Addie's heart flinched at the image of living without Johanna. She wondered anew how such tragedy could have engendered sweetness rather than bitterness in Cordelia. She doubted she herself had done as well with her losses. Sometimes she felt as hardened by circumstance and practicality as the women who robbed the dead after battles.

Even as Cordelia flirted playfully with the men, she was patient with Rand's bid for his share of her attention, complimenting him on the handsomeness of the frog he brought to show her, but reminding him that the creature shouldn't be out of the water too long.

Rand nodded gravely and said, "Uncle Hart told me he ate some frogs in the swamp, well, their legs anyway." He made a face and eyed his uncle suspiciously.

"He won't need to eat your frog," Cordelia assured him, stifling her laughter at Hart's blush at being found out for boyish bragging to his nephew. "He's getting plenty of good food to eat here; he doesn't need to add frogs and toads to his plate."

Hart drew himself up in mock outrage. "The French consider frogs a delicacy, and we did not eat toads! And don't ask me why not, young man, we just didn't."

"I know why, 'cause you get warts on your tongue if you eat 'em!" Rand told him with all the superiority of a child who has discovered ignorance in an adult. He skipped off to put the frog back in the water.

"So there, Uncle Hart," Cordelia said, sounding no older than Rand, and they all laughed.

But the illusion that the war was far away could not be maintained. Cordelia was still there when a neighbor brought the welcome news that Arnold had returned to New York and that Cornwallis seemed to be preparing to quit Williamsburg. However, where Cornwallis was going was a puzzle, and Justin and Hart worried that he would return to the Carolinas to try to win back what they had taken from him; a potent threat because it would unite his divided army.

July 4, the anniversary of the signing of the Declaration of Independence, was a somber day despite efforts to remember the promise of it, for the bold words were five years old, a lifetime away from that euphoric time when the enemy had been driven from Boston and the Continental Army was in possession of New York.

Though they pled with her to stay, Cordelia left the next day, and Addie knew it was because Justin and Hart were also preparing to go, and Cordelia wanted their family to have the last hours with them.

"Thank you," Addie told her. "Thank you for the return of the brother I remember from long, long ago."

"No, the gratitude is mine. This is the first time I have felt anything at all since my husband and our children died." Her face twisted with grief, and she stopped, swallowing convulsively to control her emotions. When she turned to bid farewell to the others, her smile was in place. "Do not let those Carolina ladies make you forget what you have in Virginia," she chided both men, but her eyes lingered on Justin, and a long look passed between them, as if they already knew how to speak intimately without words.

Four days later, Justin and Hart left, too. Once a ways down the river, they would reclaim their horses, left hidden at a fellow officer's farm, and ride on south until they caught up with Harry Lee again.

"Keep safe," Addie murmured, holding very tightly to Justin before she let him go.

"And you," he said.

She watched until the deepening shadows of the summer night had engulfed the small craft. But even when Justin was long out of sight, she could still see the bleak weariness in his eyes, all trace of Cordelia's swain gone. He hated the savagery of the war in the South, but he was going back to it because his loyalty and honor demanded it. With her fear for him, she felt an equal measure of pride that he, Ad, their cousins, and all the others like them were holding fast years after the first confidence of victory had passed. This seasoned courage was a weapon as dangerous as any blade or gun, made more lethal because the enemy, even after so great a time, refused to credit it.

The next morning, Johanna, after looking around for her uncle, asked in her new babble, "Gus? Gus?"

This time, Addie could not hide her tears from her daughter.

Chapter 4

Summer 1781

In Philipsburg, New York, Matilda pretended not to notice that Ad had reread his sister's account of Justin's visit to Castleton so many times, the letter was shredding, and she ignored his uncharacteristic shortness of temper. She shared his impatience. Indeed, she thought almost everyone in Washington's army was as ready to explode as a badly cast cannon. Even her usually calm brother, Luke, had developed the annoying habit of cracking his knuckles nervously, as if he could not find enough for his hands to do.

Every day Ad worked on letters, dispatches, and plans for an attack on New York. He knew how much the general wanted to take the city, and he thought Washington wanted it even more because of Arnold's return. But it was a worthy target, Arnold or no. If the Americans could recapture it, the British would lose their major garrison and finest port, and would be left with only a few strongholds in the South. And it seemed a safe assumption that any concentrated attack on New York would cause Clinton to call in troops from the South, thereby easing the situation for generals Greene, Lafayette, Wayne, and von Steuben and their men.

Since learning about an American loss that resulted in the near destruction of Wayne's troops at Green Springs Farm in Virginia, and about Justin's visit to Castleton, Ad had grown more frantic to be with his siblings. He went so far as to consider resigning from the staff so that he could go to Castleton or join Justin, but reason insisted that, especially now with Hammy gone from headquarters and John Laurens still absent, Washington's need for seasoned aides, particularly those who spoke French, was greater than ever. Even Lafayette, whose English grammar had steadily improved, preferred to send dispatches in French and trusted Tench and Ad to translate them accurately. It would be as difficult to leave Tench as to leave the general.

Feeling as he did, it was hard for Ad to accept Hammy's actions. After leaving headquarters in May, Hammy had pursued his own interests, but was now back with the army, in command of a battalion of New York troops in the light infantry. Hammy had long desired a return to an active field command, and Washington had been magnanimous in allowing him to retract his resignation and in granting him what he wished. Ad did not feel so generous toward him. Hammy was no longer part of the staff, and the endless work at headquarters was a constant reminder of how much his services were needed.

But it was not only a determination to fulfill the obligations of his loyalty to General Washington and to his fellow aides that kept Ad in place. It was true, though irksome to admit, that there was little he could do at Castleton and that the last thing Lee's Legion needed was a man so lame he could not ride as fast and far as the legion's maneuvers required.

Everything depended on the French, on more French troops, sailors and ships. But as yet, there was no certainty that either were on their way, despite the pledges. After all the meetings and correspondence, and even though Rochambeau's army had been encamped with the Americans at Philipsburg for the past month, there was still no definite plan to attack New York. Meanwhile, the French ships under the command of the Comte de Barras remained at Newport, Rhode Island.

The Comte de Rochambeau was ever affable and appeared to defer to Washington, but he made no secret of his preference for a campaign in the South rather than against New York. It was not wholly unreasonable, as Southern waters were more accessible to the French ships, which were to come from the Caribbean. But Ad thought it was more than that. Rochambeau simply did not believe that Clinton's garrison had enough weaknesses to justify an attack, not with British ships in the harbor and prowling the coast. Ad had the uneasy feeling that the Frenchman was right, and he was haunted by images of the inevitable carnage were an attack on New York to fail. Five years had not dimmed the memories of Quentin's death on Long Island and the scramble of the Continental Army to get out of New York with the enemy in close pursuit.

When a letter from Darius came through the lines, Ad's first reaction was that it must contain dreadful news about Darius himself or about their father. But Darius was well, resettled in his New York life, on parole, and waiting for the official exchange that would allow him to return to the fighting. The purpose of the letter was contained in a brief passage.

> *I regret I did not do this a year ago when I first became aware of your circumstances. Now it is done. Henceforth, all Valencourt properties in Boston belong without restriction to you, Justin, and Addie. You are not to worry about what our father might think about this. He has been in England for a long time, and he left me to make the best decisions I can.*

The letter included documents to underscore the legality of the property transfer, as well as excerpts of letters written to authorities in Boston assuring the same thing. The book and stationery store and the printing office, the wharves, and other real estate Marcus had owned—all of it was awaiting the return of Lily's children. It gave Ad a feeling of permanence that he had lacked since leaving Boston. With work, he, Justin, and Addie could rebuild the various enterprises. They would not be impoverished, and he could provide for Matilda. Then he realized something else: Darius had no faith that the British would ever recapture Boston; he had seen no reason to provide for such an eventuality. Ad could not know whether his half-brother imagined living in a country forever divided or if he was losing confidence that the British could maintain the few strongholds left to them. The one thing certain was that Darius was not so naive as to believe that avid Patriots and agents of the Crown and Parliament would ever again coexist in tranquility.

But Ad was not cynical enough to believe that Darius's motives were only practical. The short message from him was enough to explain that the disposition of the properties was being done because he thought it just, and out of affection for Lily's children. And surely having Addie and Silas in his life for those months and having Justin save his life at Fort Grierson had strengthened those bonds of the heart. Darius's ability to look beyond their political divisions made him an exceptional man, and Ad wished their father could have learned from him, not for the matter of property, but for the admission of affection.

Ad had not yet found the time to write to his siblings about Darius when electrifying news reached headquarters—the French fleet commanded by the Comte de Grasse was sailing for Chesapeake Bay. The period of indecision was over. If there was to be any major campaign against the enemy this year, it would take place in the South, not against New York.

The dispatches had come in on August 14 and 15, and a week later Washington's army was on the march. The general was leaving behind a force of twenty-five hundred to keep an eye on Clinton, but two thousand Americans and four thousand French soldiers would travel more than four hundred miles overland.

Although their duties multiplied, Ad, Tench, and the other aides understood all over again why they had placed such trust in Washington for so long. When the dispatches concerning the French fleet first arrived, the general was as much disappointed as elated, for they put an end to his dream of attacking New York. But he was swift to put his disappointment aside, and he turned his energy toward deceiving Clinton. In spite of the size of the operation, he intended that Clinton know nothing of it until the troops were well away, so that the enemy could not make an attempt to destroy the enterprise before it began. To this end, he ordered bread ovens be built in Chatham, New Jersey, as if the French were to have a permanent encampment or were to attack Staten Island from there, underscoring the illusion by making sure that French soldiers in their unmistakable uniforms were visible. And as he had before, he entered gleefully into the game of feeding false information to the enemy.

Ad and Tench labored over elaborate plans for an attack on New York that would never come, and the general, with Tallmadge's able help, made sure the lies flowed in a steady stream to Clinton's headquarters. Nor was Washington's own army told of its destination for the first days of the march, which, as it proceeded across the Hudson River at King's Ferry and then south, would have been the same were the army going to attack Staten Island.

They would be traveling hundreds of miles, and Ad was gratified that Washington did not suggest he stay behind. The General knew how anxious he was to go South. And Ad was wise enough not to suggest to Matilda that it would be easier for her if she did not accompany the army.

Matilda was so accustomed to following the army, she was packed and ready to leave within hours of Ad telling her where they were bound. Because he would be ahead with Washington's suite and she would be with the women and children in the baggage train, she knew they might be separated for most of the journey, but that did not trouble her. Luke would be with the main body of the army, so she was sure to see him now and then. And both Ad and Luke were so filled with excitement and hope, it was enough that she would be with them when everyone reached Williamsburg.

Ad left with the taste of Matilda's sweet kiss on his mouth and the image of her wide smile.

"I suggest you marry Matilda before one of the rest of us decides to court her. She's as good a campaigner as any soldier I know," Tench teased as they rode away.

Ad surprised himself by saying, "If this venture is successful, I will marry her by Christmas, if she is still willing."

"No doubt of that. We all envy the way she looks at you." Tench heaved a theatrical sigh.

"And what about your Anna Maria? Is she willing?" Ad asked slyly.

Anna Maria Tilghman was Tench's cousin, though he had met her only two years ago, and despite his attempts to be discreet, more than once he had betrayed his growing interest in her by questioning fellow Marylanders who had been home and might have news of her.

"I hope she will be if we ever have enough time together to learn about each other and if she does not choose another in the meantime."

Tench so seldom showed any discontent with his long service, his exasperation reminded Ad of how fortunate he himself was to have had Matilda beside him for more than three years.

Washington moved his own swiftly to allow for the French to follow closely, but the French, possessing large amounts of baggage and equipment, crossed the Hudson much more slowly than the Americans, causing the general to fume at the delay. But eventually all were across the river and on their way.

Though no enemy troops attempted to impede the march, civilians turned out along the route, many holding small children high in their arms, making sure they saw General Washington as he rode by. It was a moving display, for the people showed a grave respect for the commander in chief, as if they were blessed by his passage. The French officers were fascinated and impressed by this, and Ad overheard one saying to another, "The King would give much to command such affection from his subjects."

"Ah, but this is not commanded, it is given," the other man observed.

Washington had planned to make as much use of waterways as possible; at Trenton boats were to carry them down the Delaware to Christiana. From there they would have a march of only twelve miles to Head of Elk at the northern end of the Chesapeake. However, when they arrived at Trenton, there was such a shortage of boats, there were scarcely enough to transport the baggage. But the general was not going to allow this setback to sway him from his purpose. He and Rochambeau conferred, and the Frenchman graciously insisted that whatever room there was after the baggage had been loaded should be filled by American troops. It was decided that the rest of the Americans and all of the French would continue overland via Philadelphia.

Washington left General Lincoln in command and set off with his aides for Philadelphia at so brisk a pace, officials there had little time to prepare for his arrival, despite the efforts of express riders to deliver the news as quickly as possible.

Though his throbbing leg would have welcomed the respite of a boat ride, Ad was not altogether sorry about this development, because he thought it would be good for members of the Congress and the citizens of the city to see the general. Indeed, from the time his suite arrived on the afternoon of the thirtieth to be met by a cavalry troop and escorted to the City Tavern, the round of social and political observations began, with members of Congress and various other prominent citizens visiting.

For temporary headquarters, Washington was the guest of Robert Morris in the elegant Morris residence on Walnut Street. Morris's appointment by Congress as superintendent of finance was as recent as February past, but the merchant and former member of Congress had long been the most eminent financier of the war, having understood always—and pressed the point—that wars could not be fought with ideas alone. Washington liked the man and he was grateful for Morris's unflagging efforts to provide for the Continental Army when too many others seemed to think the men should fight hungry, naked, and unarmed. Rochambeau and his staff received their own welcome, lodging with the French minister, Chevalier de La Luzerne.

Ad was given leave to spend the evening with Hartley, and he and his uncle passed a pleasant time visiting the Birdsalls. The last time the Birdsalls had seen Ad, he had still been struggling to walk and ride with any assurance. Now, though he was stiff and sore, he seemed so much improved to the couple, they were as pleased as if he had learned to fly.

Chloe Birdsall fretted that Matilda could not join them. "Poor dear, trailing behind in all that dust and heat. When she arrives near the city, you must arrange for her to come in for a rest."

"Thank you, I will do that," Ad promised.

The evening was particularly enjoyable for Ad because Uncle Hartley appeared less haggard than he had in years, as caught up in the excitement as anyone.

"My boy, if Washington can vanquish Cornwallis, we will have them! The British people will not tolerate the loss of another army. As much as the war has cost us, so has it exacted a high price from them."

Ad thought of his father and wondered if Marcus would ever see any price as too excessive for the return of British rule to America.

He did not speak of that, but he told his uncle about the property arrangements Darius had made.

Hartley said, "He knows they are finished. But more, he knows you belong in this country, and he does not."

Ad had thought the same thing, but nonetheless it made him sad to hear someone else say it.

The next day, Washington addressed the Congress. His words were brief and dignified, evidence of his gracious spirit, for though the Congress had caused him innumerable problems over the years and continued to be miserly in practical support when he most needed it, he did not reprimand them.

"He is having to beg for help to feed our army while the French can purchase what they need with their hard coin, and yet he deals gently with the Congress. It is well I will never hold such an exalted position," Ad told Tench, "for I doubt not that I would lack restraint and belabor them with the hell they deserve."

"And receive even less help from them," Tench said.

When Washington walked through the streets, a crowd followed, as hungry for the sight of him as those along the route often had been, and the city celebrated his presence with guns firing from the ships on the Delaware and with torches illuminating the darkness after the sun had set. That night there was a feast at the Morris mansion for both American and French dignitaries, which kept the French-speaking aides busy.

Lavish toasts were exchanged, and if many shared Ad's view of how odd it was to be drinking to "His Catholic Majesty, the King of France," a monarch who allowed his subjects far less freedom than that granted to the subjects of King George III, copious amounts of wine eased the awkwardness.

Though the festive air continued in the city, the next day brought serious news to the general. To the good, Clinton had not discovered Washington's departure until it was too late to do anything to disrupt it, but a British fleet of twenty warships had left New York. The ships could be going out to make sure the French vessels under de Barras could not sail south from Newport to join de Grasse's incoming fleet, or perhaps they were sailing toward the Chesapeake. De Grasse had more ships, but if the British reached the bay ahead of him, they might negate that advantage because room to maneuver for battle would be much more limited than on the open sea.

It was very frustrating to Washington and his staff that they lacked so much information. They did not know whether de Barras had sailed, or where precisely de Grasse was at the moment, or the true object of the British fleet. It was intolerable to imagine that by the time the American and French forces completed their march to Virginia, Cornwallis might have been dangerously reinforced or carried to safety on British ships and there was nothing they could do but continue with their plans.

Ad had his own cause for frustration. Hartley, with his customary efficiency, had located Matilda, who was now, he assured Ad, settled at the Birdsalls. Ad received the news at midday, but it was late in the evening before he could get away. The Birdsalls' house was only a short distance from the Morris residence, but by the time he arrived, it appeared the household had settled in for the night. Having been with Washington's advance party for the entire journey, Ad had not seen Matilda for nearly two weeks, and he had to fight the temptation to batter on the door until someone admitted him. Instead, he went back the way he had come, trying not to dwell on the fact that if he and Matilda were married, it would have been perfectly proper for him to have gone to her no matter what the hour.

The next day, the general took pity on him, sending him away with mock sternness to "fulfill your social obligations." Ad didn't question how he knew Matilda was in the city; he was accustomed to the commander's attention to every detail.

Ad found Matilda in high spirits and anxious to stroll in the city with him in spite of the oppressive summer heat. But she was forthright in her concern for him.

"If your leg is causing you too much discomfort, we could settle in the Birdsalls' garden."

"No, I am all right," he assured her.

She didn't push the subject further, though his limp was worse than usual and pain lines framed his mouth. She understood that he had grown so used to being in pain, he could hardly remember what it was to be free of it. She swallowed hard against sudden tears.

When he told her he had tried to visit the previous night, she confessed, "I had hoped you would, and I tried to stay awake, but I'd had a bath and wonderful food, and the bed was so soft, I closed my eyes just for a moment, and then it was morning."

He was a trifle piqued to think of her sleeping peacefully while he longed for her, and she read him easily.

"When one travels with the Continental Army, one must be very practical," she reminded him. "And we were so long with the Birdsalls, it seems as if they are family of a sort." She paused, and then she said, "I do not miss you at night," and paused again, causing Ad's heart to plummet before she added, "any more than I miss you during the day. Day or night, I miss you every second of every minute when we are apart, except when I dream, because in my dreams we are always together." She spoke as calmly as if she were discussing the boats on the river.

Ad stopped midstride, holding on to Matilda's arm so that she halted, too, causing pedestrians behind them to check themselves and mutter in annoyance. He drew her out of the traffic and into the shade of a big chestnut tree. He looked down into her face, which was alight with love and mischief, and he kissed her with no regard for the reaction of the staid citizens of Philadelphia. She kissed him back with equal fervor, and he saw her more clearly than ever before, saw how much she had grown in confidence, sure enough of herself and of him to return his love in full measure, free of reservations about the differences in their backgrounds. Her clothing was as threadbare as was that of most of their army, and she was without artifice, but he had never seen a more beautiful woman.

"Christmas," he said when he could draw breath, and at her look of bafflement, he explained, "I want us to be married by Christmas, no matter what happens in Virginia."

"All right," Matilda said without hesitation.

He didn't care that he could not foretell the outcome of the Virginia campaign or that their situation by December might be as precarious as ever. Nor had he any intention of leaving the general's service if he were still needed. No longer could the conditions that had so long constrained him to a sensible course outweigh his desire for Matilda. He was not like Hammy; he would not allow marriage to deter him from duty.

He kissed Matilda again. "We will be content together, I promise it."

She murmured, "We already are," right before his mouth found hers once more.

Belatedly he realized they must be shocking more than a few observers. But times had changed. Most of the passersby were continuing on their way, and the few who paused for a closer look at the couple showed benevolent approval of the tall, young Continental officer and his lady.

Reluctantly, Ad bowed to the demands of time, escorting Matilda back to the Birdsalls' before he returned to duty. Doubting he would be able to visit her again, he began to discuss provisions for her to leave the city, but she cut him short.

"Don't fret. The Birdsalls and your uncle have everything in hand, and I will see you in Williamsburg. Do not drive yourself too hard, you—" she stopped herself at his look of amusement. "Then let us lie and promise that neither of us will worry about the other."

"We come to such easy truces, we will of a certainty deal agreeably in our marriage," Ad told her, and he went off whistling to receive Tench's good wishes for his bold action and for Matilda's willingness to match it.

The next day, some of the American troops paraded through the city. The soldiers had sprigs of evergreen in their hats, but there was no way to disguise the ragged state of their uniforms, and with no rain having fallen for days, a blizzard of dust rose up around them, adding further disrepute to their clothing. But they stepped lively to the fifes and drums, past the crowds of well-dressed, well-fed spectators. So had the soldiers marched through the city before the disaster at Brandywine; it was to be hoped that this time they were heading for victory, not defeat.

The French were encamped outside the city and were scheduled to parade through on the following day, and in contrast to the Americans, they were earning praise and fascination for the sheer beauty of their uniforms and the precise drills they were performing for visitors. Nonetheless, some of the Frenchmen were so eager to show their support by marching with their tatterdemalion allies that extra guards had to be posted to keep them in their camp.

Ad, watching the Americans passing in review before General Washington, would not have traded a single one of them for a regiment of French soldiers. Even the general's horse seemed to understand the dignity of the moment, standing so still for his rider that the two of them appeared to be a magnificent statue.

Some of the men had begun to grumble when they had found they were heading for Virginia, and the seeds of mutiny were ever a danger when soldiers were so ill-provisioned, but their respect and love for General Washington were apart from these dark currents. With typical American impudence, some of the frontiersmen referred to him among themselves as "Old Hoss," but no offense was intended; the nickname, and others like it, were just a way to claim Washington as their own, though he was a Virginia gentleman and they were from less civilized regions.

As he had feared, Ad left Philadelphia with Washington's party without seeing Matilda again, but there was no help for it, and he knew her to be capable of continuing the journey without him.

At Chester, Delaware, news reached them that de Grasse's fleet had arrived off the mouth of the Chesapeake, and the aides witnessed an amazing transformation in the general. All somberness fell from him and he was nearly delirious with joy. Knowing that Rochambeau and his staff had secured a boat at Philadelphia and were soon to arrive, he rode to the wharf, dismounted, and waited. When the boat hove into view, Washington began waving his handkerchief in one hand and his hat in the other, and shouting the grand news across the water. And in an even more astonishing display, when Rochambeau was ashore, Washington threw his arms around him.

To see the general behave in this manner sent such a wave of tenderness through Ad that though there were comic aspects to the scene, he felt like weeping, and when he glanced at Tench, he saw that his friend was having the same struggle.

The good tidings spread rapidly, and when the army reached Head of Elk, Washington wrote an order announcing the news officially and calling upon his officers and "the brave and faithful soldiers… to exert their utmost abilities in the cause of their country, to share with him the difficulties, dangers, and glory of the enterprise." And a few days later, he was able to see his soldiers given one month's pay in silver. Robert Morris had struggled mightily to get the loans to pay it, and the news of de Grasse's arrival had made it possible. It was so little for the men, but compared to so long without pay at all, or with pay in nearly worthless Continental paper, the hard coin took on a significance beyond its actual value.

Because both of his horses had gone lame, Tench left his post with promises to catch up as soon as he could. He proposed to head for the Eastern Shore of Maryland, where he had friends and kinsmen who would help him. Ad hoped Tench would have a chance to see Anna Maria, but he doubted it, for Tench was loath to be absent from his duties a moment longer than necessary.

For his part, Ad wished he were doing as well. His mare Ember was continuing sound, but his own leg was protesting the long journey so viciously, sometimes he had to hold on to the saddle after he dismounted lest he disgrace himself by crumpling to the ground. He was grateful that his fellow aides pretended to notice nothing amiss, though one or another of them just happened to be close whenever he got down from the saddle.

Baltimore gave Washington, accompanied by Rochambeau, a wild welcome with cannons firing and illuminations lighting the city after dark. Every official seemed to have a toast to propose and a speech to give, and the general received their plaudits with patient grace. But the next morning, while the sky was soft before the sun's rising, Washington and his aides were riding hard away from the city, bound for Mount Vernon, with Rochambeau's party to follow on the general's invitation that they visit his home.

The aides' excuses were that the general had always been a man who could outride or outdance any other and that they wished to spare themselves and their mounts a sixty-mile race, but when they fell back and saw Washington ride beyond their sight with only his steward Billy and one aide to represent them all, the unspoken truth they shared was that he deserved at least a small private interlude with his wife and the people of Mount Vernon on his first visit home in more than six years.

Though the aides slowed their pace enough so that they did not reach Mount Vernon until the following day at dinnertime, the slower pace did not prevent Ad's leg from becoming so badly cramped that after he dismounted, he couldn't take a step on his own. To his chagrin, he had a friend on each side, the two acting as a pair of crutches, when the general and his lady appeared to welcome the new arrivals.

"I beg pardon for presenting myself before you this way, Mistress Washington," he said.

Martha brushed his apologies aside, murmuring, "My poor boy, let us make you comfortable," and before he could protest, he found himself ensconced in a chair with his leg propped up as if he were an elderly man suffering from the gout while the activity of the house swirled around him.

He chafed at this special treatment, even as he was grateful for it, but it was impossible to reject the hospitality of Mount Vernon. With its splendid views of the nearby Potomac River, it was a fair country seat, and despite the general's long absence, his plans for expansions and additions to the mansion continued to be carried out under the supervision of his cousin, Lund Washington, and Martha, when she was not with the army in winter quarters. Likewise, the land was carefully maintained, and Ad and the other visitors were beneficiaries of this, with produce from the gardens still in great plenty, along with meat, fowl, and fish.

Before sunset, Rochambeau and his staff arrived, and on the next day more of the French contingent came in, as did Tench, who appeared late in the day, disheveled from his hurried trip but satisfied to be riding one sound horse and leading another.

The house was overflowing with visitors, and much of the talk was of war, the subject that bound them all together, but that did not dim the quiet pleasure the general was experiencing from being home. He smiled often, conferred with his cousin about every aspect of the estate, and looked on his wife with such pride and contentment, Ad wondered how he could bear to leave her again.

Besides the military visitors, Martha's son by her first marriage, Jacky Custis, his wife, and their children had joined the party, having come from their home, which was not far distant from Mount Vernon. Though Jacky was a rather spoiled man who seemed much younger than his twenty-seven years and was closer to his mother than to the general, the general was enchanted with the children and with their mother Nelly, who had become very important to Martha.

Observing him in this setting, the country squire surrounded by people and acres he loved, it struck Ad anew how much of himself Washington had given up for their country. He wished the general could have a longer pause at home, but after just three nights in his own bed, Washington was heading south again. And the aides counted an addition to their number, because Jacky went with them, bedecked with a green riband his mother had found for him that he might be properly identified, though he had not regular uniform. It was late in the game for him to volunteer his services, and his mother and his wife were at once reluctant and proud to see him go. Whatever his private opinion, the general accepted his presence amiably, because to indulge Jacky was to please Martha.

"If our prospects continue to improve, I wonder how many more gentlemen will appear to enjoy the coup de grace," Ad muttered to Tench, thinking more of Hammy than of Jacky, and was immediately sorry for his comment.

"Feeling a trifle resentful, are you?" Tench asked.

Ad conceded a fair hit, then he looked more closely at his friend as they rode along. After the care he had received at Mount Vernon, his leg was so much improved, he did not worry for himself about the rest of the journey to Williamsburg, but he was not so sure about Tench, who looked exhausted, his skin sallow, as if he had a fever. But when Ad inquired about his health, Tench made light of it, referring to not having seen Anna Maria while he was in Maryland.

"What you behold is a man beset by frustration."

Knowing the futility of pursuing the subject, Ad let it drop. Keeping up with the general was a test of endurance for everyone.

On the afternoon of September 14, two days after they had left Mount Vernon, General Washington, the Comte de Rochambeau, and their aides rode into Williamsburg. Guns saluted the arrival, and American and French soldiers turned out to honor their commanders. There followed a reception of welcome, a fine supper, and a musical offering by a band that played part of a French opera.

For Ad, Williamsburg evoked such nostalgia, he felt as if around this corner or that he would see Addie and Quentin as they had been seven years ago when they had last visited Virginia together, and as soon as he was able, he planned to go to Castleton, willing to make the journey for as little as a few hours of Addie's company.

In the meantime, it was reassuring to see the American and French officers behaving so cordially toward each other, and it was a special pleasure for Ad and the other aides to witness the fierce joy of generals Wayne, von Steuben and Lafayette that they no longer had to battle Cornwallis alone. Despite the long struggle, von Steuben had lost none of his exuberance, but Wayne was suffering from gout and from the effects of a leg wound he had gotten from one of Lafayette's pickets who had mistaken him for an enemy when Wayne was coming in to join the main force. Lafayette himself was shaky with the ague that had confined him to his bed for these past days.

But when Lafayette spoke to Ad, he insisted there was another cause for his debility. "Mon ami, it is not the fever, it is old age that makes me so weak."

Ad struggled to maintain a serious demeanor but lost the fight and laughed aloud. The Frenchman's distress about the birthday he had had just over a week ago was such common knowledge, Ad had heard of it within a short time of arriving in Williamsburg.

"My dear marquis, if you are ancient, then so am I and my sister, for we have both been twenty-four-years old for months longer than you."

Lafayette scrutinized him as if to discern the ravages of age. "Perhaps you but never the fair Ariadne." The marquis paused as if reluctant to broach a delicate subject, and when he continued, it was in French to avoid any misunderstanding. "As we are speaking of family, I remember that the family of your mother has a house in this village. The enemy was here before, and then we came, and some of my officers have been there. I hope there is no damage, but it would be best that you go to make certain of this."

"Yes, I'll do that," Ad assured him. "I meant to go anyway. I have happy memories of that house before the war. But I saw it from the outside today, and nothing appears amiss."

The marquis was not content with that. "You will go soon, to see inside?" he asked, still in French, and Ad promised he would.

There was an odd look in Lafayette's eyes, causing Ad to suspect that he already knew there was considerable damage to the house but didn't want to tell him. His heart sank; the Castletons were fond of their Williamsburg residence, and he particularly disliked the idea of having to tell his aunts that their home in the old capital was another casualty of war.

The evening's festivities ended at ten, and Ad was bone tired, but there would be a full day's work to face with the new dawn, and Lafayette had planted the seeds of urgency in him, so as soon as he was off duty, he went to the Castleton house. As Washington was staying in the home of a friend, George Wyeth, on the west side of Palace Green, it was a short walk to the Castleton house on the east side.

The first thing he saw was that in spite of the late hour, there were candles in the downstairs windows, a heartening sight after the darkness that had deterred him from visiting Matilda at the Birdsalls' house in Philadelphia. He realized Lafayette hadn't been specific about the officers staying there or whether they were there still, but he assumed the candles indicated the house was occupied by more than the few servants who cared for it in the family's absence.

He knocked and waited. The door opened, and for an instant, he was frozen in place, staring at the slender woman illuminated by the candle she carried.

"Addie?" he croaked.

Very carefully, because her hands had begun to shake, Addie placed the candlestick on a little table near the door, and then she launched herself at him, his name a glad cry.

At first he was so glad to see her, he simply held her. His voice was choked when he finally managed to say, "There are no officers in the house. Lafayette knows you are here."

"Indeed. We arrived only this morning and paid our respects to him. Poor man, he has risen from his sickbed just for General Washington. He promised he would contrive to send you here, if not tonight, then tomorrow. He was as gleeful as a schoolboy anticipating your surprise. We did not wish to distract you until the day's ceremonies were over."

Ad's mind began to function again, and he heard the anxiety under the excitement in his sister's voice. In the past, he would have expected her to do this, to appear in the midst of things with little regard for her safety should the enemy not be contained. But she was a mother now; her daughter the center of her universe.

"We? Johanna is with you?"

She shook her head in negation against his chest and stepped back with a little sigh. "No. Sissy and I came together, but Rand and Johanna are at Castleton. Too many contagions travel with the army to risk the children's health." She took his hand. "Come, let us be more comfortable." She led him to the best parlor, where two chairs and a small table had already been pulled away from the wall and arranged in anticipation of his visit. There was a small stack of books on the table indicating how Addie had passed the hours waiting for him.

He was considering how he would find time to spend with her and their cousin when the truth swept over him, and he understood her nervousness and the true cause of her being in Williamsburg. In the dark shadows of the room with only faint candlelight, vision was obscured, but he saw her clearly.

"You did not leave your daughter that you might see me," he said slowly. "You knew I would manage one way or another to come to you at Castleton. You are here for him, for Colonel Traverne."

"Yes, for Iain, the father of my child, the man I love. He is there with Cornwallis and the rest. My loyalty has not changed. I want General Washington and our army to triumph, and I believe we will. But I need to know how Iain fares. I would that he and his people survive to go home to Scotland."

Ad could not allow the silence to stretch between them. "Because of you, I want that also. Your Iain and Papa, and Darius as well, have much in common. They are honorable men caught in a dishonorable cause. And you and I seem to be vastly attracted to Scots."

It was the highest accolade Ad could grant to Iain, not only that he would equate him to their father, but that he would also see a parallel with his own love for Matilda.

The tension flowed out of Addie as she asked, "Matilda, where is she? Surely you have not left her behind!"

Ad threw up his hands in mock defense. "I would as soon try to hold back the sea. She is coming with the main army, and yes, I will bring her to you as soon as I can. I'm pleased to tell you that whatever happens, we will be married by Christmas."

"Oh, that's wonderful!" Addie exclaimed in delight, but she grew serious as Ad went on to explain what Darius had done regarding the Boston properties.

"It is a great relief to know that we will not be destitute, that I can provide for Matilda."

"How odd that it is Darius who gives us a plausible future when his own is in doubt. How strange that we have come close to him because of the war that divides us," Addie said softly.

Despite the excitement of seeing his sister, exhaustion was beginning to overwhelm Ad; his leg throbbed, and he craved the oblivion of sleep, but after a brief inner debate, he decided there was more he needed to tell her.

"We have had news of the French fleet, and I expect it is true," he began cautiously. "The French are reported to have routed the British fleet and sent it scurrying back to New York. If that is so—"

"Cornwallis has little chance," Addie finished for him. "I hope it is true. I hope for anything that brings a swift end to this misery."

Her calm acceptance reassured him.

"I share your hope," he said, stretching cramped muscles and swaying slightly as he stood.

"Can you not stay for a good night's rest?" Addie asked.

He declined. "I must return to headquarters. There is much to do, and I should be within call should the general begin his day before dawn."

She walked with him to the door, and he drew her close and kissed her on the forehead.

"Though it might have been wiser had you stayed at Castleton, I am glad you are here for whatever reason. I have missed you mightily this past year and more."

"And I you." She watched him until the night swallowed him, but even when he was out of her sight, she could feel the strength of his presence. Despite their long separation, he was still as much a part of her as her own soul.

Chapter 5

Fall 1781

The French victory at sea was confirmed and, as hoped, Admiral de Barras had brought his ships and troops from Rhode Island, sailing into Chesapeake Bay while de Grasse's fleet was out battling the British, so that when de Grasse returned, the combined French fleets numbered thirty-six ships of the line, nearly twice as many as the enemy's and a guarantee that the British would not seek to renew the naval engagement. In addition to the land troops aboard the ships, de Barras was also transporting Rochambeau's siege artillery.

In the meantime, the American and French troops coming overland had found, as at Trenton, a shortage of boats at Head of Elk, necessitating that most of them continue by land rather than being transported more quickly and less arduously by water. Some troops had not yet gotten even as far as Head of Elk, with the result that the line of march stretched over many, many miles. But they were coming, and as long as Cornwallis was stranded at Yorktown with the negligible support of a small garrison eastward across the York River at Gloucester Point, Washington did not have to press the attack before all the troops and guns had arrived.

The General's greatest concern was that de Grasse would depart early with his fleet in order to avoid the storm season on the American coast. If the French fleet were gone, Cornwallis would have a chance of rescue by the return of the British fleet from New York. In order to foster good fellowship, three days after their arrival in Williamsburg, Washington and his staff set off to visit de Grasse's flagship.

Ad was part of the group, and he told Tench, "Now you will all walk as I do—unsteadily." But he worried about being away from Williamsburg for fear that Matilda would arrive while he was gone.

"You will be back soon enough," Addie reminded him before he departed, "and if you leave word at headquarters for her to come to me, all will be well."

To her great relief, when Ad had escorted her and Sissy to headquarters for a visit, they had both been warmly welcomed by the general and his staff. The officers had inquired after the health of Addie's child, and there had been no awkwardness in it. With the pattern long established of officers' wives being with the army only during winter quarters, the men were accustomed to the sporadic nature of their time with them and to the women's lives, including the birthing of children, going on away from the war—Kitty Greene's journey to deliver her child at Morristown having been a defiant exception. Further, Addie was aware that it favored her situation that Johanna was not before them for any to think her too young to have been fathered by Silas, though most of them, particularly the bachelor aides, would have found it hard to judge any child's age precisely. Most importantly, the men genuinely wished Addie well and were pleased to see her again.

Ad was as relieved as his sister at his fellow officers' reception of her and knew he did not have to hover over her to protect her from insult, nor was it solely his concern for Matilda that fueled his reluctance to leave the town. Since it seemed unmanly, he was not about to admit the true cause to Addie, but he was bleary-eyed from the combination of work and the constant social round of shared meals and endless toasts designed to strengthen the bond between allies. At least in Williamsburg he had the chance of interludes at the Castleton house where Addie and Sissy let him rest and did not urge another glass of strong drink upon him. He thought this campaign might turn him into an abstentious man, for though food was in short supply due to armies having traversed and occupied the area for months, there was no lack of spirits. He shuddered inwardly at the thought of the toasts that would certainly be drunk aboard the *Ville de Paris*, and despite his jest to Tench, he hoped he wouldn't disgrace himself by his clumsiness.

Ad had a little time to find his sea legs, for when Washington and his party embarked on a launch sent by de Grasse to transport them, they had quite a distance to travel down the James River and across the bay to reach de Grasse's anchorage on the ocean side of the Chesapeake. It was early the following morning when they beheld the impressive sight of more than thirty ships at anchor, their masts a forest on the water.

The *Ville de Paris* was the grandest vision of all, reputed to be the largest warship in the world. When they went aboard at noon, they were greeted with great ceremony, but the solemnity was suddenly broken as Admiral de Grasse rushed up to Washington, embraced him, kissed him on both cheeks, and exclaimed, "Mon cher petit general!" Unlike most Frenchmen, de Grasse was tall, a match for the general's great height and much broader with the evidence of good living, and even allowing for French flamboyance, it was extraordinary to hear him addressing Washington as "my dear little general."

Ad covered his rising laughter with a cough, and he heard others near him doing the same, but General Knox was overcome by mirth and laughed out loud. His ruddy face turned redder, his big belly shook, and his amusement was so contagious, little ripples of laughter spread out among those around him.

Ad doubted Washington was as amused as the rest of them—this being a serious occasion and His Excellency being conscious of his dignity before these Old World aristocrats—but at least he did not look angry. Knox's outburst contributed to the atmosphere of bonhomie that prevailed during the visit. De Grasse's orders were to stay until mid-October, but he agreed to extend the time to the end of that month. Washington was pleased with that, though he failed to persuade the admiral to send ships up the York River past Cornwallis's stronghold to further trap the enemy, nor would de Grasse agree to cooperate against other targets, such as Charles Town, if Yorktown were swiftly taken. But considering how undependable French naval support had proven in the past, it was just short of miraculous that the ships and troops were here now and prepared to cooperate against Cornwallis.

When the meeting was over, Washington's departure was delayed because it seemed that every officer in the French fleet wanted to pay his respects and bid adieu to the general. The launch waiting to carry him back to Williamsburg took on the aspect of a floating reception as the officers climbed down the side of the *Ville de Paris* to board the much smaller vessel, but finally only the passengers remained, and the return voyage could begin.

But even then, the French were not finished with the day. On the tall masts, sailors balanced as sure-footed as monkeys, holding their muskets and firing them one after another in a feu de joie. Cannon roared over their salutes, and the smoke of the gunpowder was tinted rose and gold by the sunset.

Ad was tired from bracing himself against falling, from the toasts he had dreaded, and from translating French into English and vice versa for hours, but the fierce beauty of the scene caught at his body and his soul, filling him with new energy. Matilda might be in Williamsburg by now, and he longed to see her and to describe what he had just witnessed.

However, to the frustration and acute discomfort of all aboard, it was four more days before they were back in the town, and by then they had suffered headwinds, no wind, drenching rain, and roiling stomachs.

As they disembarked from the launch at last, Tench said, "Your prediction has proven accurate. We are all reeling, even His Excellency."

When they arrived back at Williamsburg from the river, it was to discover that most of the trailing American and French troops had come in to the encampments, with those yet to appear following close behind. And to Ad's relief, there was a message at headquarters that Matilda was with Addie. He went to her as soon as he could, and though he had done his best to brush his uniform and generally make himself presentable, he knew he hadn't done a very good job of it when Matilda flew at him with a host of anxious queries.

"Are you all right? Oh, you look pale, and the sea clings to your clothes! What delayed you so long? You are never to go on a boat without me again, never!"

He silenced her with a kiss and observed, "This is backward. I expected to welcome you, worn and wan from travel; instead, I come to you as something the fishes would not want."

"Well, I want you," Matilda said, still giving him wifely little pats, as if to reassure herself that he was truly before her.

Addie and Sissy had kindly allowed the two a private reunion, but all three women gathered to hear Ad's tale of the visit to de Grasse. He gave such vivid details of the tributes paid to Washington and the enthusiasm for him among the officers, Addie got a lump in her throat, but she was entertained, too, thinking of the hugely stout Henry Knox roaring with laughter when everyone else was trying not to.

Ad was not so amused when he heard about the women's activities in his absence. There were makeshift hospitals that had been set up for those suffering from a variety of complaints, in the main injuries and fevers, and the women were visiting the sick, doing what they could to alleviate their suffering. Their activities had attracted attention, particularly from French officers who seemed to Ad to be appearing in ever larger flocks to proclaim their undying admiration for the American ladies. The fact that Addie was fluent in French was hailed as a gift directly from God, but Ad didn't think it would have made much difference if the women had been mute in all languages. The situation passed beyond his understanding when Cordelia Wakefield Armacost joined the household with a warm welcome from Addie and Sissy and quick acceptance as a new friend from Matilda, who already felt as if she'd known Sissy for years and was enjoying the company of the women.

"You should not be exposing yourself to the dangers of the hospitals," Ad protested righteously to his sister. "And what is Cordelia doing here? I remember when you couldn't abide the woman."

"As for the hospitals, we have all been caring for the sick for a long time; Matilda and I with the army, and Sissy and Cordelia on their plantations. And as for Cordelia, Sissy and I feared her when we were girls and she was a woman, but now we are all adults, and Cordelia has survived more sorrow with more grace than anyone I know. She isn't here to flirt with the pretty French officers; none of us is. Cordelia and Sissy are here because they are Virginians and Americans, and they want to see the enemy gone from their land."

She was tempted to tell Ad that Cordelia was also hoping to see Justin, no matter how unlikely that was, but what had begun between Cordelia and Justin at Castleton was so new and fragile, she would leave it to Justin whether or not Ad should know. Instead she said, "You know where my heart is and that Matilda's is in your keeping. You have no cause for jealousy. But I confess to you that it is diverting to be paid such extravagant court. It is all foolishness, but it makes us feel young and beautiful, as if the war were far, far away, not just down the road."

Ad could not think of any further objection he could raise without sounding churlish, because no matter Addie's explanation, he was jealous; he wanted other men to be blind to Matilda's charms. The sheer selfishness of the thought shocked him, and worse, his twin read him clearly, but she treated him gently for it.

"You must understand. Each compliment Matilda receives, she receives as proof that she is worthy of your love."

He could not resist this female logic that offered such reassurance, but he said, "War is much simpler than dealing with women."

"Which accounts for why men are so eager to march off and leave the women behind," Addie remarked tartly. Then her mood darkened. "It will be very soon now." She did not need detailed information from headquarters to know that. "You will send word if you learn anything about Colonel Traverne?"

"I will." As he agreed, he felt a deep pull of sorrow for her. If all went well for the allies, the best news there could be of Colonel Traverne was that he had survived to be among the defeated.

Only a few days later, on September 28, Ad left Williamsburg with the allies, both armies under the command of General Washington. The French and Americans marched in good order through countryside that was lush but overgrown and nearly devoid of its usual inhabitants, the houses derelict. But as they neared their destination, they passed the sight of huddles of slaves trying to hide in the woods; men promised freedom by the British and now cast out so that they need not be fed from dwindling supplies; many of them dying of smallpox and other diseases; some already dead, and the odor of decay tainting the air.

The sounds of an army on the move—the tramp of feet and hooves, the creak and rumble of wagons, the jingle of spurs and bits, the music of fifes and drums, the steady hum of voices—all came from the French and Americans. Of the enemy there was no sign until the allies were in sight of Cornwallis's stronghold and saw some cavalry parading, but a few shots from the allies' guns sent the horsemen galloping for shelter. Cornwallis had made no attempt to interfere with the march. Instead, it was apparent to the naked eye that the British had concentrated their energies on fortifying their position.

Yorktown seemed a poor choice to go to ground, cut off from supply lines and perched as it was at the point of land where the York River emptied into Chesapeake Bay. Nor was it much help to the enemy that they also held Gloucester Point cast across the river, for those troops were being watched by a mixed force of French regulars and Virginia militia, as, on the west side, Washington moved into position to prevent any escape by land from Yorktown. The only possible deliverance for Cornwallis was by water and required either going north on the York River or rescue by the ships of the British Navy that had been turned back by the French.

Ad felt some faint pity for the British commander. The intelligence the allies had received over the past weeks indicated that Cornwallis had been charged with establishing a base for naval operations in Virginia, rather than being free to devise a plan wholly to his benefit. He had gone to Yorktown with far more possibilities open to him than remained. He had surely believed earlier on that Clinton would send more troops and ships to him, and he could not have foretold that, after the previous failures, the French fleet would not only appear in a timely manner and in great strength, but would succeed in driving off his salvation.

That first night Ad and the other aides slept on the open ground near the general, who had chosen a spot under a mulberry tree, using the root for his pillow. It made it seem as if it were the early years of the war again, and Ad marveled anew at the endurance of this man who was nearly fifty years old. But things were not as they had been, not even among the staff. There was Hammy, off with his light-infantry troops, cordial toward his old friends but no longer part of headquarters. And the same was true of John Laurens. He had arrived in Boston late in August, had gone to Philadelphia to address the Congress regarding his mission in France, and had then traveled on south to Williamsburg to join Washington's army. His fellow aides credited and congratulated him for helping to speed assistance to them by his effort at the French court, and he had been as pleased to see them as they were to have him back.

Ad had taken him to see Addie, who had immediately asked if his wife had contrived to visit him in France.

"She did, and she brought our daughter, little Frances Eleanor, to meet me; such a remarkable child, so beautiful and intelligent, though she is only four years old," he had boasted, as if he were the most devoted of fathers. "Perhaps someday soon your daughter and mine can play together when it is safe for my little family to come to the United States."

But despite this evidence of domesticity, John was not tame enough to return to regular headquarters duty, albeit he was willing to serve as a secretary when needed. His participation in the futile campaign to keep Charles Town out of enemy hands had given him a keen taste for action, and though the appointment to France had been laudable, it had been far too civilized for his taste. He wanted to be in battle again; most of all, he wanted to return to South Carolina to chase the enemy from Charles Town, a wish made more fervent by his father's continued imprisonment in England.

Ad shied away from a too careful inspection of his disquiet over the changes in the staff, wanting to put it down to the general's need for support from dependable aides, but in honesty, he had to admit that his own need was great. With Marcus long disappeared to England, with Quentin and Silas dead, and Justin riding with Lee's Legion, Washington's "family" had become his. These men meant so much to him that any departure meant the loss of a friend and brother. He wanted them to stay together for as long as they could. Because of Darius's generosity, a plausible civilian life awaited him at war's end, but even when he reminded himself that Matilda would be beside him, it was hard for him to imagine quiet days as a bookseller and printer in Boston. There was guilty relief in reminding himself further that the war was not over yet.

In the first days after their arrival at Yorktown, the armies' encampments began to take on a more formal appearance with careful attention to staying out of the range of the enemy's guns. Tents were erected, including the general's big marquee. General Knox's guns were still on their way over bad road and swampy ground that made for slow progress, and there was much to do before they were placed. But Cornwallis had already done a great deal for the allies when he had surrendered the surrounding countryside without opposition, even withdrawing his Yorktown outposts the second night of the allies' appearance before him. He had apparently decided to await reinforcements well behind the works he had had constructed.

The fortifications were impressive, making the best use of natural as well as man-made obstacles. A swamp on the right and a deep ravine on the left would hinder movement and, in the center, the front trees of a thin wood had been chopped down, branches facing outward so that getting through would be like traversing the densest underbrush. And as if this were an ancient city in the Old World, walls and redoubts had been constructed to command every land approach to Yorktown. There were more batteries in the town itself, and the vessels still at Cornwallis's disposal were anchored in the York River and armed.

The tasks for the allies were straightforward. First the engineers would determine where best to place guns to fire on the enemy, and then entrenchments would be dug in the chosen ground parallel to the enemy fortifications so that the batteries could be erected therein. Then the contest would begin—Washington's guns against Cornwallis's.

The general was methodical in his planning, relying on the French engineers with siege experience. His one serious remaining worry was that Cornwallis would contrive to escape northwest on the York River and thence overland. Despite his continued pleas and Lafayette's, the general could not persuade de Grasse to bring his ships up the river past Yorktown to block the way. But even were Cornwallis to utilize this route, he would still be in grave trouble. The York River was not the vast Chesapeake; it would not carry the enemy far before the ships would have to be abandoned and the troops marched on land, where they would once again be vulnerable to Washington's huge army, for while Cornwallis's force was estimated to be around seven thousand, the allies now numbered more than sixteen thousand. After so many years of fighting irregular battles against superior numbers, it was a most complete reversal of fortune for the general to have such an impressive army at his command and to be executing a formal siege so dear to the workings of European armies.

Although there had been some brief exchanges of small arms fire with the enemy, the allies had as yet made no response to the cannonade from the Yorktown defenses, and Ad wondered if those inside the stronghold had been lulled into believing they would be spared an answering bombardment. For most of the allies, it was easy enough to judge the range and stay out of the way of enemy shells. Only those who ventured too close to the enemy or who were working on the entrenchments were in danger, and to make those men harder to see, much of the digging was done at night, even through the rain.

Beginning on the night of October 6, the first parallel trench was opened and construction of the redoubts needed for safety was started. The enemy took note of the activity and increased the cannon fire, but day and night the work went on, with men and cannon being placed until by October 9, enough of the batteries were ready for Washington to touch off the first gun at three in the afternoon. It was one of the French guns, aimed by French artillerymen, and the cannon ball pounded into the enemy's fortifications exactly where it was aimed. More French guns were fired with the same accuracy. Three hours later, some of the American batteries joined the action. They proved it was well that Washington had done his symbolic duty with a French gun and had deferred to the expertise of French engineers and gunners since the beginning of the siege, for many of the American shots landed willy-nilly, and some also failed to explode. It was somewhat embarrassing, but understandable, as the French guns and munitions were far newer and of much better quality than those of the Americans. Ad doubted that it mattered that some of the American shots were going wild. The roar of the allies' artillery was unceasing, going on through the night, joined by more guns in the new day, and due to increase further as additional batteries opened.

Nothing in the long years of war had prepared Ad for the sounds and sights of the siege. He was transfixed by the rumble of guns and the thudding impact of cannon balls that made the earth shiver as if in a constant, frantic dance to throw off the armies upon it; by the explosions of the howitzer shells that continued to cause little jolts to his nerves even after he thought he should be used to them; and by the insidious music of so many missiles rending the air. He thought he would hear that sound between a whisper and a whine, even were he to go deaf from the loud explosions.

By the light of day, the sight of the cannon balls crisscrossing each other in the air as both sides fired simultaneously was memorable, like the work of jugglers gone mad. And the night scenes were magnificent. During the day, the bomb shells were black spheres, but at night they became lethal fragments of the heavens, falling stars and meteors arching up, glowing red, then streaking toward their targets, trailing tails of light.

No matter how accurately the artillerymen strove to aim their guns, some of the shells went beyond the town to land in the river; throwing up spouts of water, and in the night, a red-hot shell set fire to the *Charon*, a British ship of forty-four guns, and to small vessels around it. The *Charon* became a skeleton of fire, rigging and masts delineated by flame while the false stars continued to fall from the sky. The thunder of the guns was so loud, even those close by could not hear the crackle of the conflagration or any screams that might have come from seamen trapped aboard.

But if the cannonading at night took on the aspect of a vast theatrical production, the reality was revealed by sunlight. After seeing detached arms and legs flying into the air in the wake of an exploding shell, Ad tried not to focus too sharply on the points of impact.

Through it all he and the other aides kept up their mundane tasks, allowing no reaction to the bombardment to jar their pens or splatter ink as they kept up the neat clerical work of war.

"General Greene could use some of the troops and ordnance you have in such good supply here. If you will write out the orders, we'll be on our way."

Ad put his quill down hastily before he could spoil the page he was working on, and then he was up, stumbling in his haste, and Justin's arms came around him, steadying him as they embraced. They hadn't seen each other in nearly a year and, for a moment, neither could trust his voice enough to speak. Thereupon, Justin was engulfed in a flurry of welcome from Tench and others, and he greeted them in turn.

He told his brother, "Harry Lee and the others are with His Excellency. They sent me over to surprise you."

"You've certainly accomplished that!" Ad exclaimed, knowing he was grinning like an idiot and not caring. "I had no word of your coming. Is the whole legion here? Is—"

Justin was smiling, too, as he held up a hand to stem the flow of questions, but he sobered as he explained. "The legion is with Greene. Harry Lee, Hart, Reeves, a few others, and I really have come to beg prettily for men and arms and anything in the way of supplies that His Excellency can send to us." His eyes narrowed at the memory of what he had seen riding in. "Christ's blood! I didn't know there was so much lace left in the world, let alone gold lace."

Though Addie had told him how worn Justin had looked when he had come to Castleton, Ad was shocked by the change in their brother. Justin had always been slender, but now he was honed so fine, his shabby uniform hung on him. His face was tanned from the sun, but the color did not hide his underlying pallor and it drew attention to the amber of his eyes. He looked like a lean, dangerous wolf made into a man, and Ad understood the current of anger running through him. As the two of them left the tent, he saw the encampment through his brother's eyes. The American troops were as ill-clothed as ever, though some of the officers had managed to keep up their personal toilettes, even to lace cuffs, frilled shirt fronts, and smartly cocked hats. But the French were dazzling in their bright white shirts, vests, breeches, and stockings or gaiters with contrasting coats of rainbow colors indicating their elite regiments. Their coats were dark blue with rose, sky blue with yellow, red with yellow and white, on and on, many with such luxurious details as embroidered fleur-de-lis on the white turn-backs and gold piping glittering in the sun to match the gold lace on hats.

The officers were noblemen with perfectly powdered hair, garments of the finest fabrics, and the appearance of courtiers on their way to the palace at Versailles rather than soldiers on a field of battle.

In the distance, they could see the general, accompanied by aides and staff officers, Harry Lee's small party, and Rochambeau and his staff.

"They are conferring about the second parallel. It must be opened soon," Ad said, and Justin nodded. "I heard that much before I rode over to find you."

"The French are vital to this campaign," Ad reminded him gently. "It is their money, men, guns, ships, and their engineering skills that are making it possible for us to be here."

"I know that." Justin sighed wearily. "Harry Lee has been sure all along that Cornwallis could be taken if he came north to Virginia. But it is so frustrating that Greene's army lacks everything we need to finish the job in the Carolinas and Georgia. We need the French fleet to support us in attacks on Charles Town and Savannah, but we aren't going to get it, are we?"

Ad resisted the urge to give him false hope. "No. His Excellency and Lafayette were barely able to convince de Grasse to stay in our waters to the end of the month. He will not tarry for another campaign. But surely the general will send reinforcements to Greene when this is finished."

"They won't be enough." Justin's shoulders slumped for an instant, and then he straightened, gazing toward Yorktown. The thunder of the guns was continuous, cannon balls visible in the air like a deadly plague of deviant insects. "I would not want to be in the enemy's position," he murmured, and Ad heard the echo of his own sympathy.

"Addie's in Williamsburg," he said.

"Has she no sense? I would have thought with Johanna—"

Ad cut him off. "Johanna is safe at Castleton. Our sister would not risk her health, not even for—"

It was Justin's turn to interrupt as understanding dawned. "Not even for Johanna's father." He looked toward the fortifications again. "So Colonel Traverne is there, poor bastard. And poor Addie, too."

"At least she is not alone. Sissy came with her, and Matilda is there. But the most extraordinary thing is that the ever beautiful and once despised Cordelia Wakefield Armacost has been welcomed into the fold as the best of friends!'

"Cordelia's in Williamsburg?"

To his astonishment, Ad saw his brother transformed from wolf to lamb by the mere mention of Cordelia.

"It's like that, is it?" Ad could not hide his smile. "I misunderstood. I thought you were cured of a fever at Castleton, not that you contracted one there."

"Perhaps both," Justin admitted. Ad was regarding him indulgently, and Addie had obviously kept his secret, so he could not be angry with either sibling. Suddenly it was a relief to speak openly. "I need to see her again. I can scarcely credit that she is as lively and beautiful as I remember. Maybe the fever affected my perceptions."

"Or your heart," Ad suggested. "It sounds like the same affliction I have long suffered because of Matilda. I hope I will never be cured of it!"

The arrival of the general's party put an end to the brothers' conversation, and Ad was swept up in a round of greetings from his cousins, Harry Lee, and several others who had come north. It was peculiarly comforting to note that all of them, even Harry Lee, who had always been so fastidious about his personal appearance, looked worn-out by the arduous campaign in the Carolinas. This evidence of shared hardship made Justin's condition seem less alarming to Ad. And he would have thought they would all be grateful for a respite, but to a man, they were impatient that because they were officially under General Greene's command, as a courtesy to Greene, Washington would allow them no part of the action at Yorktown, and they had to content themselves with acting as observers.

"There is little for you to do anyway, unless you want to join the artillery," Ad pointed out to his brother. "Why don't you request permission to visit Williamsburg?"

Justin refused the suggestion on the grounds that it would not be fitting to leave the siege. But he changed his mind and decided to go with them when his cousins announced their intention to visit the town.

"If anyone is going to lay siege to Cordelia's affections, it is going to be I," he told Ad.

Within a few days, Ad wished he could have gone with them. The establishment of the second parallel was not going as smoothly as had the first. This entrenchment was halfway to the main British line, and on the right, nearest the river, the position was within range of two advanced enemy redoubts armed with guns that were doing a good job of stalling the completion of the works. Ad had no quarrel with the decision to storm the redoubts, but it was hard to know that both John Laurens and Hammy were to be part of the attack, while he himself would be tamely waiting for news of the success or failure of the venture.

It was hardest of all to face his resentment toward Hammy. To Ad's mind, John had never faltered in his service to the cause, but Hammy had deserted for his own interests and was now back and insistent that he be allowed a role in the action. Grudgingly, Ad had to admit that Hammy was eligible to take part in the assault. Eligible, Ad's mean spirit carped, only because Hammy had been allowed to retract his letter of resignation, thus retaining an unbroken record of service.

Ad knew Tench was aware of his troubling reaction to their old comrade's assignment, but Tench did not pressure him about it, and Ad did not wish to discuss it with anyone. But the conversation went on in his mind, and in spite of all his efforts to convince himself that Hammy was overbearing and vainglorious, finally he had to admit that the greater fault lay in himself. He was jealous on a most basic level. Hammy moved with the lithe grace and strength needed for the swift action being planned, and Ad saw too clearly the contrast to his halting gait. He would be naught but a liability were he to go with Hammy and the others. He had thought himself resigned to his lameness and knew he was fortunate to have kept the leg at all, so it was discouraging to discover that there was still part of him that longed so much to be as he had been before being wounded.

In preparation for the storming, the batteries blasted away at the two redoubts during the day of October 14, with the attack scheduled to commence in the evening. A French force of four hundred would go against one of the redoubts; an American force of equal size would go against the other; and Hammy was to lead that assault.

Washington positioned himself on a small rise where he could view the action, and Ad was there with other aides and staff officers, including generals Knox and Lincoln. He wondered how many of the watchers wanted as fiercely as he did to be with the waiting troops, blood singing and every muscle tensed in anticipation of the order that would send them forward, and he thought ruefully that His Excellency was surely one of them.

"Sir, you are too much exposed here. Had you not better step a little back?" one of the aides asked.

Ad was glad it was not he when the general snapped back, "If you are afraid, you have liberty to step back."

They stared into the darkness, and then the six French cannon shots sounded in a predetermined and unmistakable, odd rhythm. The night exploded in covering fire from the allies, and in a desperate flurry of musket flashes and blasts of artillery from the British line trying to protect the redoubts. But the attackers were going in with bayonets at the ready, and the sounds of close combat were audible—the grunts and shouts of great effort, and the screams of the wounded. Then, after only fifteen minutes, the Americans were cheering their success, and a few minutes after that, the French were doing the same from the position they'd won as the enemy fled for their lives.

Even as the wounded were being carried out, work parties and engineers poured in like ants to finish the second parallel, to fortify the sides of the captured redoubts that faced the enemy, and to mount two howitzers in each that would be able to fire ricochets, so that cannon balls would speed along at ground level, hitting a multitude of objects and bodies with each shot. The enemy tried to reach the workers with artillery, and some were hit, but most of the shells were aimed too high, evidence of how ill-prepared Cornwallis had been for the night's attack.

Both the Americans and the French had suffered casualties, but Lafayette, John, and Hammy were not among them, and Ad breathed a sigh of relief, admitting to himself that he would have felt a superstitious guilt had Hammy been injured or killed. Equally important, no enemy had been harmed after surrendering; Tarleton's Quarter had not been permitted by the officers, though it might easily have been invoked by the men, who had a new rallying point for vengeance.

Every soldier now knew that in early September, while the allies had been marching south, the traitor Arnold had led a devastating raid on the port of New London, Connecticut, burning the town and allowing the slaughter of the entire garrison of Fort Griswold across the Thames River from New London, though the vastly outnumbered men in the fort had tried to surrender. That Arnold had his origins in Connecticut made the destruction seem particularly heinous, the man beyond salvation.

Before dawn there was a brief alarm caused by cries in the darkness and some firing when the enemy made an attempt against the center of the second parallel, but it was over by the time the general was mounting his horse. The sortie had been so certain of failure, it was taken as no more than a gesture of defiance from Cornwallis, who was in the worst possible straits with the allies' bombardment continuing at closer range, pounding Yorktown to bits.

In selfless proof of his dedication to the cause, Thomas Nelson, Jr., the current Governor of Virginia, had directed the gunners to correct their aim in order to hit his own residence in Yorktown because he was sure Cornwallis would be using it for headquarters. And now stragglers from the town were claiming that Cornwallis was living underground, in an earthen den. It was harsh enough that there were soldiers in the village, but it was worse that civilians remained, too. Ad did not want to imagine what it must be like for them with everything being smashed around them and death falling from the sky and rolling along the earth.

Justin returned with their cousins from Williamsburg and shook his head in appalled wonderment. "I am glad Addie can't see this. Any word about Traverne?"

"No. How is Addie faring?"

"You know how strong she is, and no matter what happens, she will go on for Johanna's sake. She misses her very much, and that she had not returned to Castleton is a measure of her..." He hesitated only briefly. "... love for Traverne. For it is that. She loves him for his own sake, not just because of their child. Her heart has been tried enough in this war. I pray he survives."

"And your heart?" Ad inquired, hoping he was shifting to a more pleasant subject.

He was rewarded by his brother's smile.

"As lost as I had suspected." Justin carried with him the image of the blaze of joy on Cordelia's face when she had first caught sight of him. "She is not as I remembered; she is more. I think Mama's blood may win in the end; I think I may become a true Virginian." Justin watched Ad's face as he said it. Ad had told him about Darius's transfer of the Boston properties, but Justin could no longer picture returning to life there, to the city where Sarah had died, not when Cordelia's life was so deeply rooted in Virginia.

"I see," Ad said without heat, because it was true. He had his doubts about returning to his old life, and though he was grateful that Matilda seemed willing to live wherever he chose, if she were not, if she insisted on returning to McKinnon, he would go with her, no matter how alien the life was there. But nonetheless, it was hard to think of being so far from Justin even after the war ended, and he flinched away from the pain of it.

They had their first direct news of Colonel Traverne the next morning when the enemy counterattacked against the two most forward allied batteries, spiking guns and killing some French soldiers. But as brave as the action was, it was of no lasting use, the cannon being quickly restored to service. Colonel Traverne and some of his Highlanders had been part of the force, but reports of the skirmish had it that the Scots had gotten back to their lines without severe injury. By French descriptions, in the dim glow before the dawn, Traverne had loomed a huge, savage man with a visage made terrifying by the scar he had gotten at Guilford Court House, a veritable monster of a man.

"Addie had better not hear him depicted so," Ad remarked to Justin. Both of them were infinitely relieved that they did not have to report Traverne's death to her.

"Damn Cornwallis!" Justin swore. "It's over. Any further delay is no different than if he lined up his men and shot them himself."

That night, a storm roared over them, so wild and loud it made the cannonade seem puny. The squall subsided, and daylight revealed British boats on the York River and Cornwallis's desperate attempt to escape. He no longer had enough boats to carry his army up the river, but he did have sixteen good-sized oared boats that had not been sunk or burned by allied shells, and he had tried to ferry his troops across in relays to Gloucester Point. From there, if they could have fought through the militia and French troops posted to watch the Gloucester Point garrison, his army could have marched away overland, though to what end, no one knew. But the storm had served as Washington's final weapon. The boats seen in the morning light and targeted by allied artillery marked the last of the troops being carried back to the doomed town.

On the morning of October 17, the fourth anniversary of Burgoyne's surrender at Saratoga, a red-coated drummer boy appeared on the enemy's parapet and amid the smoke and thunder of the guns, he began to beat the chamade, the long roll that called for a parley. Then an officer waving a white handkerchief came forth from the enemy works, and the guns fell silent.

It was a silence so profound that when the officer advanced with the drummer still beating the message, Ad thought he could hear their footsteps louder than the pulse of the drum.

The terse message from Cornwallis to Washington read:

Sir:

I propose a cessation of hostilities for twenty-four hours, and that two officers may be appointed by each side, to meet to settle terms for the surrender of the posts of York and Gloucester.
    I have the honor to be sir,

Your most obedient and most humble servant
Cornwallis

The terms General Clinton had dictated to the Americans after the fall of Charles Town had been harsh, and now Cornwallis was to receive a taste of the same with the public ceremonies of surrender, but in the basic provisions of the capitulation, Washington strove for fairness. Though army and naval stores were to be turned over to the Americans and the French, officers would keep their side arms, and officers and soldiers both were to retain their private property of every kind, and no papers or belongings were to be searched. Slaves would be returned to the properties they had left.

The biggest problem was the prisoners. The war was not over, no peace treaty had been signed, and the allies could not afford to risk setting so many free on parole or sending them back to Europe, where they could relieve soldiers there who could in turn be available for duty in America. Instead, the soldiers were to be kept in Virginia, Maryland, and Pennsylvania, as much by regiments as possible, and all were to be provided with food and clothing the same as soldiers in the Continental Army.

"Well, that should keep them naked and hungry until they go home," Justin muttered as he copied out articles. Though the guns were silent, musicians on the two sides were exchanging salutes with every instrument they had, from fifes and drums to bugles, French horns, and bagpipes. The music provided a background for the furious scratching of quills at headquarters. Chafing with inactivity, Justin had volunteered his services to help as the Articles of Capitulation were worked and reworked, copied and recopied.

This duty the general allowed, saying with a wry smile, "I think General Greene cannot fault me for discourtesy in this, for you should not come to harm with pen and ink." Justin understood the general's generosity in letting him do this for his own contentment, though he had abandoned these secretarial tasks long ago.

"With Burgoyne's soldiers still in our keeping and now Cornwallis's, we can hardly afford to win another such victory unless the enemy pays swiftly for their care," Ad said. He stared at the wording of article six, which allowed the general staff and other officers who were not to serve as field officers with the prisoners:

... to go on parole to Europe, to New York, or to any other American maritime posts at present in the possession of the British Forces, at their own option, and proper vessels to be granted by the Count de Grasse to carry them under flags of truce to New York within ten days from this date...

"What do you think Colonel Traverne will do?" Ad queried softly, so that other aides would not overhear.

"I don't know. He's a staff officer, but he's also devoted to his Highlanders. It will be a hard choice, but surely the wisest course would be for him to go home. Whatever power and influence he has to effect an early exchange will not serve him here."

Neither of them ventured a choice because neither of them knew what would be better for Addie—to have Traverne gone away forever, or to have him somewhere in the country so that at least there was some small chance she would relent and go to him with the truth about Johanna.

"It makes it much harder that he is an honorable man," Justin said. "Unlike Butcher Tarleton—now there's a creature I'd like to stab through the heart before he escapes to his lines."

He said it with great calm, but his face was stark with hatred, and Ad had no doubt Justin would seek out and kill the man had he the chance and if honor did not forbid it. Tarleton was with the Gloucester garrison and would surrender with it, but it was a clear indication of the man's lack of character that he had ordered the slaughter of his cavalry's horses—good strong animals acquired in Virginia to replace poor Carolinian stock—rather than relinquish them in defeat. General Washington had sent a stern reprimand that had saved those remaining, but Justin and every other horseman in the allied army were repulsed by Tarleton, and it was especially embittering for Justin that Lee's Legion had not been able to capture or dispatch the Butcher in any of their many encounters with him.

"We can have little doubt where Tarleton will go. Before one of us can kill him, he'll be off to England to brag about his 'brave' exploits,"

Ad said wearily, rolling his shoulders and flexing his hands, trying to ease the stiffness.

Had Cornwallis had his way, the negotiations would have stretched out, perhaps so that rescue could come or the French depart, perhaps just because he could not face the enormity of his loss, but General Washington countered every demand for long delay by offering only brief hours, and all was in readiness for the surrender on October 19, just two days after the drummer boy had beaten the call to parley.

The day dawned with the soft, perfect brightness of autumn. Last-minute negotiations were completed, the documents signed, and at noon, the allies marched into position, the French in a line on the left side of the road, the Americans on the right, the lines extending for more than a mile.

The French appeared in all their magnificence, uniforms gorgeous, and each regiment displaying a standard of white silk embroidered with three golden fleurs-de-lis. Even their music was enchanting as they marched into place, for in addition to their fifers and drummers, they had their band, complete with tambourines that added an exotic, singing beat to the air.

The surface contrast between the two armies was great. The Americans, despite all efforts to appear as neat as possible, were still shabby, but what they lacked in uniforms, they gained in pride. They stood erect, faces alight with joy, and at the head of their line, General Washington, the big man on the big horse, was all they needed to remind them that by trusting their commander in chief for so long and by following him so far, they had come to this triumph.

The soldiers were not alone. Civilians—men, women, and children—had come from miles around to witness the downfall of Cornwallis, Terror of the South. On foot and horseback, in wagons and carriages, they seemed as numerous as the troops.

Ad was part of Washington's suite, and he did not have to crane his neck to find the women—Matilda, Addie, Sissy, and Cordelia—in the crowd. They were on horseback and had a good vantage point. He hoped Addie would not see more than she could bear. He and Justin had not bothered with so useless an exercise as sending word to urge her not to come today. But he was suffering again from sympathy for the enemy, and for Addie. He wanted Colonel Traverne to appear with enough dignity intact so that neither Addie's nor the colonel's heart was broken. Not wanting to betray any special interest in the man, he had been able to glean only basic information about him, that he had survived the siege and was not among the wounded.

At two o'clock, as stipulated in the surrender terms, the enemy marched out between the lines of the victors. To the slow, solemn beat of their drums, they marched with arms shouldered and colors cased, as the defenders of Charles Town had been required to do, though they had not been allowed any music at all. But Cornwallis was not leading them; he was nowhere to be seen. In his place was Brigadier General Charles O'Hara, who approached Rochambeau, as if dealing with fellow Europeans rather than with the Americans would be less painful, but the Frenchman would not accept the proffered sword, making it clear his troops were subordinate to the Americans and directing O'Hara to take his orders from Washington.

With that, O'Hara rode toward General Washington, doffing his hat when he was close, tendering Lord Cornwallis's regret that illness kept him from attendance, and once again offering Cornwallis's sword. Instead of accepting it, Washington calmly directed him to General Benjamin Lincoln. Cornwallis had sent a subordinate; therefore, a subordinate would accept the sword, and there could be no better choice than Lincoln, who had been the commanding general at Charles Town when the British had taken it by siege. In this reordering of the ritual, Washington showed perfect urbanity, a reminder to British arrogance that being an American did not make one a rustic.

In acceptance of the surrender, General Lincoln tapped the sword, leaving it in O'Hara's keeping to be returned to Cornwallis, and the enemy soldiers marched on to the area set aside for them to relinquish their weapons. French hussars were posted there to keep order.

With the other women, Addie watched the procession. Cornwallis had obviously turned out his stores, for most of the redcoats looked to be wearing new uniforms. But the brave display could not hide their humiliation. Some were unsteady on their feet, as if they had been drinking, and some had tears trickling down their cheeks. The Hessians were in better order. But even as she automatically noted details, Addie saw these troops as little more than shadows. Only Iain and his men were real to her.

He had disdained the superior position of being mounted on horseback. He led his men as he had through most of the battles, on foot with them. Their tartan was not so easily come by as regular uniforms, and the hard campaigning had left them as threadbare as the Americans. Some had forsaken their kilts altogether and wore trews fashioned from plaid patches, but Iain was dressed as he had been the first time Addie had seen him in uniform. The blue, green, and black tartan of his kilt, the matching facings on his red jacket, the trimming on his bonnet, and the plaid pinned to his shoulder to flow down his back—all were weathered and faded, but the touches of silver, the brooch on his shoulder, the frame of his sporran, the buckles on his shoes, and his sword hilt worked with silver and gold gleamed in the sun. To Addie, he was splendid. He walked with his head up, kilt swinging gently in rhythm to his steps. Like Justin, he was too lean; there were extra years etched on his face; and the scar from Guilford Court House was a red slash down his right cheek, but none of that diminished him in Addie's eyes.

Duncan was with him and others she recognized, but she felt the absence of Angus as an ache in her heart, and she saw how many more were missing, too. She fought to keep back her tears.

Iain had been staring straight ahead, paying no attention to the French and Americans lining the way, but he turned his head as if Addie had called his name and, for an instant, it was as if they were the only two people on earth.

She saw the shock of her presence hit him, saw his mouth silently form her name, and such joy shone in his face, she answered with her own smile, knowing her love was as plain to him as if she had shouted the words for all to hear. Then the exchange was over. His gaze was fixed once again on the way ahead, and she bowed her head to hide the longing she knew was naked on her face.

"Safely home now, my love, safely home," she whispered inside, and when she raised her head, she was in control.

But it was too late. Sissy and Cordelia were oblivious, their attention fixed elsewhere, but Matilda had seen it all, and she regarded Addie with such tender understanding, Addie had to look away lest she be overwhelmed again.

When the defeated troops reached the field where they were to lay down their arms and surrender their standards, it was too much for some of them. A colonel wept openly as he gave the commands, "Present arms! Lay down arms! Put off swords and cartridge-boxes!" A corporal clasped his musket to his breast before he threw it down, saying, "May you never get so good a master!" as if he were giving up a beloved servant or pet. And he was not the only one who tried to hurl his weapon hard enough to ruin it until all were severely reprimanded for violating the terms of the capitulation.

When the enemy troops marched back to Yorktown, some of the Americans could not resist catcalls, but no physical harm was done.

This time when Iain passed, he did not look at Addie, and she did not focus her gaze on him. It was as if they had made an agreement to spare each other the further risk of betraying themselves before their separate sides.

Her brothers were not so restrained. They sought out Addie as soon as the ceremonies were concluded, before she could escape, and they drew her away from the hearing of her companions and were clumsy in their attempts to do their best for her.

"I saw you and I saw Colonel Traverne," Ad said bluntly. "You can meet with him, you know. It is easily arranged. Now that the surrender is official, the British officers will be invited to dine with us, and we will all be very civilized, as if the carnage of the past weeks, indeed of the past years, never happened. Lord Cornwallis will, of course, have to keep to his bed for a while to maintain the illusion of the false illness that kept him from the field this day, but the rest will come, Colonel Traverne among them. It is only to their good and that of their men that they do. And thus, a visit between you and Colonel Traverne could be managed."

Compared to his spill of words, Addie's were slow and precise. "Oh, yes, what a good suggestion. In this place teeming with people, Iain, a man no one could overlook, and I, the sister of two prominent officers of the Continental Army, will meet and no one will know. No one will wonder why. No one will look at Johanna some time hence and see how much she favors her father."

"To hell with what anyone might say or think!" Justin exclaimed. "You love the man, and you have a child together."

"You are both giddy with your own loves, and I am glad for it," she said. "But Matilda and Cordelia are as American as you are, as I am, as Johanna will be. Iain is a Scot and British. If loyalty to our beliefs, to the cause, makes no difference, why have we risked so much for so many years? Why is Papa gone away to England? Why are Sarah, Quentin, Silas, James Fitzjohn, and so many others dead? If you can tell me honestly that it does not matter, I will reconsider your proposal."

While they were searching for a way to dispute with her, she added an implacable warning.

"I love you both as my life, as I love Johanna. But if you tell Iain of her existence, you will be dead to me, and I will be bereft of your comfort for all my days."

They had no answer to that because they believed her. She was a woman fighting to protect herself and her child as she judged best.

When she was out of earshot, Ad complained, "I do not relish the prospect of visiting with Colonel Traverne. We will remind him of her, and I fear the secret will bolt from my mouth."

Justin was not so downcast. "It is all to the good that we should remind him of our sister. She forbade us to speak of Johanna, not of herself. But it is Addie whom Traverne loves. Oh, yes, I saw it. They have been apart for nearly two years, but it took less than two seconds for the fire to flare up in both of them. I think that alone is proof of how strong the attachment is between them."

Ad shook his head in exasperation. "I think you are exactly as Addie said, 'giddy with your own love.'"

"She included you in that," Justin pointed out.

Ad, thinking of marrying Matilda as soon as he could, did not argue with the description.

Yorktown was a village of ruined buildings, of the defeated, the wounded, and the dead. It was also where Addie's heart abided. She did not dare to look back as she rode away with the other women toward Williamsburg. She was afraid her resolve would fail, that she would turn back and flee to Iain in her own surrender of loyalty and sanity. She could hear the evil whispers that would rise up, not just about her and her daughter, but about her brothers and the rest of the family. "And them so close to General Washington, and him trusting them like he did. Her husband not cold in his grave and that harlot lifting her skirts for the same ones who killed him."

She had gotten what she had come for—that one glimpse of Iain's survival. Her heart eased as she pictured Johanna's bright little face—a tiny, feminine version of Iain's—and suddenly she could not wait to hold her again. It was time to establish a secure life for her daughter; time to go home at last.

Chapter 6

Boston, Fall 1782

While he was still caught in the gray mist of sleep, edging toward waking, Ad knew Matilda was with him, curled warm against him, her soft scent and even breathing bringing him to consciousness with the wonder that continued to grow rather than diminish, even though come December they would have been married for a year.

He lay motionless so as not to awaken her. It was October 19, the anniversary of the surrender at Yorktown. It had been a year of change, though aside from marrying, he had not altered his course.

Washington had thanked the French and American troops as Tench had raced for Philadelphia, carrying the official news of the Yorktown victory to Congress. There had been wild celebration, and the Congress had presented Tench with a horse and a sword for "merit and ability." Ad could think of no one who deserved the rewards more. However, Ad's doubts about his friend's health had proven justified, for Tench had been ill with fever by the time he reached Philadelphia, and even after three weeks' leave with his family, he had not recovered fully. This past year he had been absent from headquarters for a full five months, and before the year was out he would be going home for good to resume his life as a civilian, although even then he would not resign his commission.

His suit for Anna Maria's hand in marriage had been accepted, and had it not been for a serious illness in her family, the couple would have been married already; now the date was set for the following June. Only Tench's certainty that the war was over enabled him to leave the general, and Ad wanted him to go that he might grow strong again. At the same time, he dreaded the day when Tench would be gone from headquarters with no prospect of return.

Lafayette was already far away, having sailed back to France two months after Yorktown. Officially he was on long leave, as Tench would be, but it was doubtful he would serve in America again. Having both public and private lives to resume, he had gone home to a family he scarcely knew, including a little boy named George Washington Lafayette, who had been born during the marquis's previous visit home.

They had all made the best of the farewells, but the Frenchman was sorely missed, particularly by the general, whose relationship with him was much like father to son.

Ad reminded himself that as sad as this parting had been, it was not as final as others. Jacky Custis, unseasoned to camp life, had caught a fever and died less than three weeks after the Yorktown surrender. If the general had not been overly fond of the young man, he had been patient with him, and Jacky was so dear to Martha, his death had been a terrible blow to her and thus to His Excellency as well. Jacky left behind his wife and four small children, and they were additional responsibilities for the general. Ad, like the other aides, had gotten accustomed to Jacky in his brief service with them, but they mourned his death more for the sake of the Washingtons' loss than for their own.

It had been quite different when they received news of John Laurens's death this past August. That was a blow deep and personal to those who had known and admired him, the sorrow made deeper by the knowledge that there had been no purpose in his death, having died in a skirmish over a few barrels of rice for which the enemy had offered to pay. His father, Henry, with whom he had had such a close bond, was still in England, though no longer imprisoned in the Tower of London, and would never see his son again. And John's daughter was now an orphan, her mother having died in France.

As he had wished, John had returned to active duty and to participate in the job of re-establishing state government in his beloved South Carolina. So well educated, so bright and engaging, he had had two flaws that together proved fatal—a raw hunger for action and an edge of recklessness that he had never fully tamed.

Hart and Reeves were still with Greene's army in South Carolina, but Justin and Harry Lee were not with them. They had left the army to return to Virginia, both of them exhausted by a stalled war and worn down by cyclical fevers that had proved such efficient weapons against friend and foe alike in the Southern campaign. Once the consummate warrior, Harry Lee had gone home to marry a cousin who not only pleased his eye, but also enlarged his fortune considerably. And Justin had gone directly to Cordelia, who by Sissy's account had been on the verge of setting off for South Carolina to collect him herself. Justin had married in May, Harry Lee in June, and both of them seemed content to train their renewed energies on civilian life.

Justin had approached his marriage to Cordelia with laudable wisdom. In spite of visits to Castleton in the past, he knew he was no farmer, while Cordelia had become a very good one, capably managing the lands she had inherited from her first husband. Justin had turned to the law, studying under the highly respected jurist and Patriot George Wythe in Williamsburg. Because of his classical education, Justin found the training easy and would soon be practicing in Richmond, which remained the capital, and therefore was where Virginia's political life was centered.

The law was the surest way into politics, and Justin's enthusiasm for both was growing by the day. He had written to Ad:

> *I am grown so weary of the chaos of war; the order of the law beckons as a refuge. And above all else, as we are no longer ruled by King and Parliament, we must establish in our towns and states, and among the states, the reign of just laws so that we do not lose in anarchy all that we have gained at such cost.*

Justin's only complaint regarding his new life was that Cordelia was prone to fussing frantically at the first sign of recurring fever. But he understood because she had lost so much to disease.

> *I have warned her that I plan to stay with her until we are both ancient and she has grown tired of my constant prattle of adoration, but she assures me no sane woman ever tires of that.*

Ad rejoiced for his brother's contentment, but at the same time he felt a peculiar estrangement from both his siblings, a matter of purpose as much as of geography, for he had not yet slipped back into a private life.

After watching the surrender at Yorktown, Addie had not lingered in Williamsburg. She had returned to Castleton and her daughter. And there Lily's children had been together for a brief time away from the war before Justin and the Castleton cousins had gone south again and Ad and Matilda had rejoined Washington's army.

Matilda had yielded instantly to Johanna's wiles, and Ad was no more able to resist her, vying with Justin for recognition as an important uncle. Addie had laughed at their foolishness, but she had also shown a steely resolve that kept them from going into detail about their meeting with Colonel Traverne.

"He is returning to Scotland?" she had asked, and when they had told her he was, her only response had been, "That is good. It is finished then." It was stated matter-of-factly, with no discernible sorrow or relief, no hint of the quick storm of emotion that had swept over her when she had seen Traverne at Yorktown. It was as if she had already moved on to a time when the Highlander was lost far in the past.

Even as Ad had understood that she had chosen this as the best course for her and Johanna, how he had wanted to describe Colonel Traverne's pain to her. The man who had led his regiment with such dignity on the field of surrender, save for that flash of passion when he had looked at Addie, had revealed much when he had spoken to her brothers.

They had seen the sudden paling of his face when it struck him anew how closely they resembled their sister, and he had made no attempt to conceal his interest, although he had been circumspect in an effort to protect her reputation.

"I saw your sister today. She appears well, though changed somehow. But of course, it was a sad time for her in New York with Colonel Bradwell's death. He was a fine man. It was my privilege to have known him, even under such trying circumstances. You will, please, give my regards to Mistress Bradwell for her continued health and happiness."

"Let us cease this play! The truth is in your child. You love our sister; she loves you. Pledge yourself to the United States, and you can have Addie to wife, your child…"

For a horrified instant, Ad had thought he'd offered the Devil's bargain aloud.

But instead, Justin had answered, "We will, and you must know that your welfare is her concern. She has told us of your great kindness and Darius's during that dark time. Your friendship is still important to her, and I do believe she came here only to ensure herself of your safety. You have friends here, more lasting, I believe, than your enemies will be. General Lord Cornwallis has lost much. Peace must come now, and when it does, the enmity toward those who fought with honor against us will begin to fade, particularly toward those willing to cast their lot with us to build this new nation."

Colonel Traverne had studied Justin thoughtfully, as if to find the added meaning in his careful words. Then he had smiled wryly and had chosen the safer subject.

"I do not fear that you will mistreat my men while they are your prisoners; I fear you will seduce them. They are loyal, but as hard as their time here has been, it has also shown them a vast country where a man might prosper if he puts his back to it."

Justin had resisted the impulse to push just a little further, to ask "And you?" And there had been no more conversation between them.

"Damn frustrating!" Justin had sworn afterwards. "I hope I planted a sharp enough thought so that it will prick his brain again and again, reminding him that he could have a new life here, an option not open to Darius and his kind, who have fought against friends and neighbors."

It was all Justin and Ad could hope for, because in January, with other high-ranking officers, including Lord Cornwallis and Tarleton, as well as Benedict Arnold with his family, Colonel Traverne had sailed from New York.

However, with the passage of time, Ad had begun to doubt that Addie needed their plotting. At Castleton, she had announced her intention of returning to Boston. "It is the most practical solution for all of us. You are still duty-bound to the army, but the properties in Boston want managing. I can do it. What I do not know, I will learn. And no one will gainsay a war widow struggling to rebuild her family's fortunes."

She had stayed in Castleton long enough to risk having Johanna inoculated against smallpox and to nurse her through the inevitable illness caused by the procedure, and then they had traveled to Philadelphia in time to attend the wedding of Ad and Matilda before going on to Boston. And here she had been ever since, seemingly content with her life and absorbed in reviving the various enterprises that had languished since Marcus had left. It was no easy task, for it was still wartime, and many commodities, once imported with ease, were difficult to acquire. But Boston had been out of direct involvement in the conflict for years now, and a semblance of normal life and something more had resumed.

Though the ships—coastal traders, privateers, and vessels from Europe—had to be wary of the British Navy, they no longer had to abide by British laws designed to control trade, and when they came in, there was Valencourt wharfage for their use, at appropriate fees. And there were goods to be obtained for Valencourt's Book and Stationery Store and for the printing office, though publications from England were so rare, it was more common than ever to turn one copy into many by reprinting, using the press Mary had convinced Marcus to store away. There were also properties for rent, easier to let now that the pace of ordinary life was increasing.

All of it was complicated by the continuing lack of hard coin and the relentless depreciation of the paper money printed by the Congress and the states, but lack of hard coin had been a problem in the country long before the war and Addie had her stepmother to thank for further easing the situation, because Addie had sold Mary's farm to the tenants who had long run it. Frugal, canny New Englanders and good farmers, they had paid a handsome part of the price and would continue to make payments for some time to come. Addie had no qualms about this transaction, believing that Mary would approve that the property had gone to help provide capital for the businesses in Boston.

From what Ad could observe, his twin was as settled as he had ever seen her. As with Justin, Ad did not begrudge Addie this new version of her old life, but it was part of the loneliness he had begun to feel with the first defection from headquarters, clear back when Hammy had left them. He and Matilda were in Boston now for only a short visit, to celebrate the reoccupation of the family home. Addie and Johanna had been living above the bookstore, but today they would move into the house on Summer Street, recently vacated by its renters. Addie figured they could afford it, and she wanted her daughter to have a garden to play in and to be surrounded by the same spacious beauty as she herself had enjoyed until the war had changed everything.

She was insistent that the house belonged to all of them, to Ad and Justin no less than to her, just as the businesses did, and that Ad and Matilda could come there to live as soon as Ad was released from duty. But nothing of his life seemed to remain in Boston, and what Addie was building seemed wholly hers. His work continued to be what it had been for all these years—to serve the general until Washington had no further need of him.

When Ad had asked permission to wed Matilda, the general had given it without hesitation, but his face, which for self-protection had grown more impassive and difficult to read with each year of being so relentlessly subject to public scrutiny, had betrayed such sorrow for an instant, Ad had been taken aback. But then he had realized the cause.

"Your Excellency, I have framed my question badly, for I ask two favors, not one. I wish to marry Mistress McKinnon and to remain in your service. She is agreeable to this, for she has been with the army for nearly as long as I."

The general had been straightforward in his relief. "Thank you. It is late in the day to find aides as loyal and skilled as you, and there is still much work to do. Peace is not yet won."

Ad and Matilda had been married in Philadelphia, with the Washingtons in attendance, because that was where the general and much of his staff had spent nearly four months, from November to March. The General had been gratified by the praise heaped upon him for Yorktown, but his chief purpose for the long sojourn in the city had been to keep the Congress from entirely abandoning the army, which was more ill-provided for than ever.

Despite the dark direction of his thoughts, Ad smiled to himself, remembering the mutual admiration Mistress Washington and Johanna had shared. Martha had been pale and wan from her recent sorrow, though as was her nature, she had done her best to put others at ease. But Johanna had charmed an answering smile from her, and nothing would do except Martha hold the baby for a while. Addie had been nervous that Johanna would change her mind and squall, but Martha and Johanna had been content in some secret communication of their own.

Watching them, the general had reverted to the Virginia gentleman, saying to Addie, "Your daughter is fortunate to be as enchanting as her mother." And far from the Washingtons or anyone else showing any untoward suspicions about Johanna or Addie, it had been more a matter of normally dignified aides and staff officers jousting for Johanna's favor, which the baby had dispensed with largesse.

Addie had observed to her twin, "Though I was certainly there at her birth, I think Johanna is Kitty Greene's child, not my own."

Ad's smile faded as he thought of General Greene, still in the Carolinas with his dwindling army short of every basic necessity. It was evidence that the war was not over and underscored the difficulty of evaluating the gains and losses of the past year.

When news of Yorktown had reached King George III in February, his response had been to call for a renewed effort to defeat what he still considered his rebellious subjects in America. But now his subjects at home were showing their own signs of rebellion. The people of Britain were tired of being at war with America and a good part of Europe; tired of the cost and of the disruption in their commerce. Yorktown acted as catalyst for the change. The House of Commons urged the King to end the conflict with America, and before a month had passed, Lord North had resigned as Prime Minister, despite the King's urging that he stay on. It would have served little purpose had he done so, for recent elections to Parliament had reflected the declining belief in the war and in Lord North's, and the King's, policy. The Tory war ministry was finished, and the King had little choice except to call on Lord Rockingham to form a Whig cabinet. Immediately, they had opened informal peace talks in Paris with Benjamin Franklin, the American Minister to France, and with other American agents there. The rumor was that formal peace negotiations would begin soon.

There were positive changes on this side of the Atlantic, too. The enemy had quit Wilmington, North Carolina, shortly after Yorktown, and this summer, after two-and-a-half years of occupation, they had evacuated Savannah, Georgia. Sir Henry Clinton had sailed home from New York in the spring, undoubtedly to protest peevishly that the bad turn the war had taken was no fault of his. He had been replaced by Sir Guy Carleton, a man of very different temperament.

Ad understood those who took these developments as proof that the war was over, but he could not ignore the negative elements. The enemy still held New York and Charles Town, and on the frontiers the summer had seen savage fighting between Patriot militia and the mixed forces of Loyalists and Native Americans. Nor was there the smallest chance that in the event of a great alarm, the Americans could once again depend on notable assistance from the French, who soon would arrive in Boston to embark on ships that would carry them away from any possibility of further combat in the United States.

Much of the Continental Army was slipping away in the resignations of officers and furloughs extended into eternity for the men because, with so little for them to do aside from watching the enemy garrisons at New York and Charles Town, with the Congress providing scant supplies, and with so much back pay already owed, the potential for harm to the country arising from the discontent of its own troops was becoming a greater threat than any from the enemy.

Everything circled back to the reality of there being no final peace treaty in place, no pledge of honor that hostilities were finally at an end. Ad was not sure that he truly believed the war could be resumed on any appreciable scale, no matter what the King wanted or how muddled British and European politics became, but the general believed it, and that was enough.

Though the slower pace at headquarters these days allowed Ad a nearly normal married life with Matilda, he thought that this might be the hardest service yet for the general; waiting to see if the war were really over; at the same time having to preside over the dissolution of the army that had so often stayed to fight only because he had asked it; and all the while having the image of Mount Vernon pulling him homeward.

"You are sad to be here?"

Ad was so tangled in his thoughts, Matilda's soft voice startled him, but then he drew her closer so she was half draped across him. "With you in my life, in my bed—sad? Never!"

But she would not be put off and propped herself up so she could see his face.

"Not sad exactly, just feeling out of place," he conceded. "And even being back in the house is not going to change that. Boston doesn't seem familiar to me anymore. I think I am jealous, for Justin and Addie have both returned to civic life so easily."

"Have they?" she asked. "Your brother and sister have found ways to be content, but I would not judge that it has been easy for either of them."

He pondered her judgment, seeing his siblings through her eyes, and it struck him that Matilda might be speaking of more than Addie and Justin. He had assumed that he and his wife were in perfect accord on this subject, but his confidence faltered, and he asked the questions, dreading the answers.

"Have I stayed in the general's service too long? Is it time for us, too, to find contentment as civilians?"

She responded instantly. "Leave the general when he has greater need of you than ever? It is unthinkable! When the time comes to leave, you will know it. And whenever that is, it will be the perfect time to decide what will be next for us."

He pulled her down on top of him, nuzzling her neck, letting the warmth of her seep into all the chill, uncertain places in his heart. She did not share either his apprehensions about what was to become of them when their time with the army was over or his periodic urgency to discover the best or worst of it. She had been exposed to a hard way of life on the frontier and in the army, and it had given her strength and a patience that he himself sometimes lacked. As important, under the strength and patience flowed more tender currents—enduring kindness and a rare appreciation of joy—and he was the beneficiary of all of it as Matilda continued to express, with heart, mind, and body, her delight in their marriage.

On their wedding night, inexperience and long denial had made their first joining clumsy and frantic, but Matilda had sighed blissfully and said, "It is well I did not know how good it would be, else I fear I could not have waited so long."

Reassured by her praise, Ad had confessed, "I think we could do with some practice," and that had become a foolish lovers' joke between them.

Matilda moved slowly on top of him, stroking his body with hers, a little ripple of laughter running through her when she felt his response. "A little practice would be a fine way to start this morning," she suggested.

"Unkie Ad and Auntie Mat wake up now? I go get 'em." Johanna's clear voice filtered into their room.

As did Addie's answer. "I think not. They will get up when they are ready."

"I am up," Ad muttered.

"But Gorgie is coming! They want to see 'im," Johanna insisted.

"They do, and they will, but you want to see him most of all, and you will, as soon as he arrives."

Ad groaned and closed his eyes as the urgency of his body faded from this intrusion of domestic affairs in the close confines of the rooms above the shop.

Matilda rubbed against him again, just to tease. "Your sister has given us permission."

"But our niece hasn't. If we have children, perhaps we should consider making them a little less bright and quick than that one."

The pride in his voice made Matilda smile. "We would be very lucky to have a daughter just like her," she said.

They were both impressed with the child and with the way Addie was raising her, for Johanna, though just over two years old, was well behaved, well spoken, curious about everything, and extremely good-natured. She had been exposed to a great many people in her short life, but no one had ever treated her badly, so she trusted the world to be a benevolent place and responded even to strangers with her own ready smile. But little George, "Gorgie" to Johanna, and his family had become favorites from her first meeting with them.

The reunion with Tullia had been something Addie had both feared and looked forward to. In January, after she was resettled in Boston, she had sent word to Tullia, finally telling her of Johanna's existence but giving no details beyond writing in the note: "I am longing to see you again, and I want you to meet my daughter."

At her first sight of Tullia, Prince, and their son, George Washington Freedom, Johanna had smiled her widest smile, clapped with glee, and announced in her most emphatic tone, "You stay here now!" And she had put her arms out to Tullia to be held.

Addie had understood immediately. At Castleton, Johanna had seen more Black people than white, had been lovingly nursed and cared for by Black women, and had played with their children. To her, their faces meant love.

There were sensitive issues between the two women, because in seeking to allow Tullia her new life with Prince without the constant pull of the old, Addie had delayed the most vital information, had not sent her timely accounts of Ad's grievous wound, nor of Silas's capture and her search for him. She had written to her of Silas's death long after the fact, and she had withheld news of Johanna's existence until she had sent the brief note. But any constraint there might have been between the women was defeated by their children.

Two years older than Johanna, George was a handsome little boy with deep-brown skin, huge brown eyes shot with gold like his father's, and a smile so like Tullia's that it caught at Addie's heart.

He had regarded her with interest, saying, "You are Addie, and your brothers are soldiers in General Washington's army, and my mama took care of you all when you were children like me."

He had looked very pleased with himself when Addie had said, "That is exactly right! How clever of you to remember all of it."

They had been lost, the two of them, Tullia to Johanna's blandish-ments, Addie to George's, and Addie had felt such a lightening of her spirit, she had wanted to laugh at Prince's expression of relief even as she greeted him.

On that first visit, the family had stayed the day, and while the children were napping, Prince had left the women with the valid excuse that he had business to attend to in the town, surely a possibility as his manufacturing smithy continued to gain reputation and orders by the year.

"I don't have to ask, I can see that life with him is good," Addie had said.

"It is so good, sometimes I am afraid," Tullia had admitted. "For all that he's big and strong, he still falls ill too often in the winter, and every time I think he's going to be taken from me. I am greedy for him, I want every second, every day into eternity with him." She had fanned at her suddenly warm cheeks. "Listen to me! It is indecent for an old woman to talk so!"

"Never!" Addie had protested. "You will never be old, and I think it is wonderful that a man and a woman can love so deeply."

"You believe that for other people, not for yourself," Tullia had observed, understanding Addie as readily as she always had. "You are not going to risk your heart again, and that is a sorrow."

Addie had not intended to reveal Johanna's true parentage to Tullia, but the words had poured out until she had stripped her soul before this woman who was as close to a mother as she had ever known.

"I thought I would find Silas again when I returned here, and I have, but only as a very young man, not as my husband. All our married life we were with the army, away from here, but when I try to bring those memories back, when I try to see him clearly, he is always dying, and even those images are fading. But Iain is clear in my mind and will be as long as my daughter is before me, as punishment, perhaps, for the joy I take in her."

"So there is no room for anyone else, nor ever will be, not as long as you have love and guilt so mixed up," Tullia had said. "Despite his difficult beginning, or maybe because of it, Silas had a generous heart. He loved you, but he wouldn't want you chasing after him into the grave. You did not betray him. He was dead when you went to

Colonel Traverne. Someday I hope you come to know that deep down inside where it matters."

"It makes no difference anyway," Addie had pointed out wearily. "Iain is on his way home to Scotland where he belongs." Belatedly it had struck her that Tullia had shown no shock at being told Iain had fathered Johanna. "You knew right away about Johanna!" she had accused in panic.

"Do not worry about it. You forget, I mothered Silas as much as he would allow it and knew him very well, and I saw Colonel Traverne when he came calling. I have all the pieces, but most people don't and won't even notice there is a puzzle."

Over the past months, Addie had learned the truth of that and of the illusions she had harbored for so long. She had known her father, Mary, and the children would not be here, but by some strange trick of her mind, she had overlooked the obvious and had assumed not much else would have changed. Indeed, Boston looked the same, there having been no great alterations made to streets or buildings or wharves during the years Addie had been gone. But the people were different. Unlike Silas, Justin, and to a lesser degree, Ad, who had all had connections with the radical Sons of Liberty, Addie, as a female member of her father's household, had developed most of her friendships among both old and young in her father's world. Not just her father, but nearly all of that world was gone, having sailed away in British vessels when the enemy had evacuated the town. And of the Patriots she had known, few were in their old places; she could scarcely imagine General Knox returning to sell books in friendly competition with Valencourt's. There were still some acquaintances, business agents, and customers, most of her father's age or older, who carried on as if the war had never happened, but there was no one who was overly interested in Addie's personal life. And as much as it was a mark of the disappearance of the Loyalists and the British officers who had frequented Marcus's shops and home, it was also a reminder of how happy she had been with Ad and the rest of her family, including Tullia and Silas, before the war, of how little she had needed anyone outside of the circle.

Over the months, as she expanded the businesses, she had grown accustomed to the personal isolation she felt and had made no attempt to modify it. After all, it was to her advantage and Johanna's, and she saw enough of Tullia to keep her from feeling completely alone. Sometimes she visited Tullia in Dedham; and there she had met Prince's grown children. They had homes of their own, but they were fond of their father, stepmother, and half-brother and spent a good deal of time with them. More than a little uncertain of how they would regard her, Addie had been shameless in taking Johanna along as a weapon on her first visit and every one since. Prince's children were still somewhat reserved toward her, but not toward Johanna, and that was enough.

It was not the same as a visit in the flesh, but Addie also had the comfort of letters from her brothers and their wives, and from her aunts and Sissy. Sissy was playing the role of Virginia matron to the hilt. After Yorktown, she had returned to Bright Oak just long enough to collect her young sisters-in-law and help them to Williamsburg. The war had deprived them of normal flirtations and courtships, and she meant for them to enjoy the rituals while she found suitable husbands for them. She had judged Williamsburg a promising hunting ground with Rochambeau's officers decorating the town, and more and more Virginia officers appearing on the scene. She was rightly proud of her town, and both girls had been married this past summer, one to a Virginian of good family, the other to a French nobleman who had won Sissy's approval for, in spite of being a younger son with a minor title, his fortune was real, and he had decided to stay in Virginia.

Sissy seemed to have no interest in marriage for herself, and Addie understood why that might always be the case. It was not only that Sissy's obligations to her son and to Bright Oak were complicated, it was also a matter of her memories of James Fitzjohn. Sissy had arranged for him to be reburied at Bright Oak, and in her mind, he was becoming an ever more perfect husband. Before long, no mortal man would be able to match him. Addie did not dwell too closely on this because it led inevitably to the suspicion that her case was worse than her cousin's, that she was doing the same with not one, but two men.

She saw Prince's buggy pull up in front of the store, and she heard Johanna's happy crow at the sight of Ad and Matilda emerging from their bedchamber. She straightened her spine and shaped her mouth into a smile. Today's purpose was to reoccupy the house with people she loved. She had already been inside the house many times, making sure everything was in order, making sure no aura of sadness filled it, even as she acknowledged the disdain with which her father would have viewed such an irrational idea. But if there were ghosts, they were no more than the benign effect of the joys and sorrows that had measured the tenure of the Valencourts. It weighed heavily on her heart, though she would never pressure Ad by telling him so, but she did not expect him to return here to live. As with Henry Knox, she could not imagine Ad settling back into the small confines of Boston. Nor would Justin and Cordelia ever come here for more than a visit unless some catastrophe swept away their existence in Virginia. None of that signified. After their years of wandering with the army, she wanted there to be a center, the security of a home awaiting any of them who might need it. She wanted it for her own secret, selfish reasons, too.

It was right and necessary that her life be as secure and well ordered as she could make it, for her life was Johanna's. Rebuilding various Valencourt enterprises and watching her daughter grow and change by the day should have been enough, but the longing for the gypsy days of following the army still possessed her too frequently. She had brought Nightingale north with her, and though she had little time to ride, when she did take the mare out, sometimes she felt as if the army were just ahead, that if she and the mare increased their pace, they could catch up to their old life. It was like craving an elixir that poisoned as it enchanted, for as much as the companionship and the sense of shared purpose, she wanted the dark side, too, the excitement that spread through an encampment before a battle, the music of the fifes and drums, the troops marching out to meet the enemy, the roar of the guns. To have seen all the maiming and death and to still want the cause—she saw madness in that, and every bastion of domesticity she could erect against it was worth the effort. Becoming mistress of the Summer Street house was a vital part of this campaign.

The bustle of the day overtook her as greetings were exchanged among the Freedoms and Ad and Matilda, while Johanna could scarcely contain her joy at having so many people she loved together at once.

Addie and Tullia had already visited the house frequently, arranging for the move, but Ad had not been inside since leaving Boston after the American reoccupation six years ago. Addie saw his apprehension just before they entered the house, but as she had on her first visit, once he was inside, he relaxed and began to look around with interest, his face softening with memory.

"What a beautiful house! But it is friendly, too," Matilda said. "How fortunate you were to grow up here!"

Ad seemed not to notice that Matilda had not made any mention of their living here, but Addie did, and out of her twin's hearing, she told her, "I mean this house to be for all of us, but I don't want it to be a burden. If you and Ad settle here, that will be well. But if you go elsewhere, that will also be agreeable." Because she had already thought it out, Addie was able to speak without betraying her sorrow.

She was rewarded by Matilda's swift gratitude. "Thank you. You know how much we both love you, and I know I could be happy in this house. But I will be happy wherever Ad is, and the choice must be his."

The Freedoms spent the night and Ad and Matilda stayed beyond that, and then Addie was left to discover whether or not being back in the house of her childhood with a child of her own would be enough to resurrect the feeling she had long since lost of belonging in civilian life.

Chapter 7

Winter and Spring 1783

In mid-December, 1782, the British had evacuated Charles Town, taking with them nearly four thousand Loyalists, thousands of slaves, and any spoils they could carry off, including silver, books, and the bells from the steeple of St. Michael's Church. Their departure marked the end of the presence of the British Army anywhere in the South.

The new year dawned, and though news was slow in coming across the ocean, as far as anyone at Washington's headquarters knew, peace negotiations were continuing in Europe. But as the foreign threat faded, the domestic danger increased. Hostilities had ceased between the regular armies, but not between the irregular bands of Patriots and Loyalists, particularly those in New Jersey, who continued to inflict violence on each other whenever they got the chance. Nor were they reluctant to harm regular soldiers when they could get their hands on them. This nasty business added strain to the uneasy truce between Washington's forces and Sir Guy Carleton's troops in New York, making it possible that some especially brutal encounter between the irregulars could spread to a larger conflict.

But of far greater peril to Washington was the growing discontent of his army. The long arrearages of pay and unanswered claims for just recompense had caused more and more indignation until in December, a committee of officers had taken a memorial to the Congress that their grievances might be addressed. But Congress took scant notice of them, and resentment continued to increase until now, in March, it seemed mutiny grew more certain by the day.

Ad would have given much to have Tench back with them for the comfort of his calm wisdom, but he had left as planned. And though there were still good men around the general, there was little any of them could do to mitigate the pain of the situation for him. It was not a rabble of common soldiers who were brewing trouble; it was honorable officers who had seen long, hard service and felt deep insult from the Congress's treatment of them. The general was in the most invidious position, for while he was in sympathy with their anger and had always tried to persuade Congress to better the treatment of the army, no defeat would be more bitter for him than if the men he had commanded took control of what fragile government there was by force of arms.

On March 10, at the New Windsor encampment not far from Washington's Newburgh headquarters, anonymous notices circulated calling for a meeting of general and field officers the next day. Worse, a well-composed address also made its way from man to man, advising that the army should take matters into its own hands, making demonstrations to instill fear in the Congress and the people, and thereby gain justice.

Ad's hands were shaking when he presented the offending papers to Washington for his attention, but it was his heart that trembled when His Excellency chose to respond in his general orders for the next day. Washington expressed his displeasure at the whole affair, labeled it disorderly, and requested that the officers, with one officer from each company and a proper representation from the staff of the army, hold their meeting to discuss their grievances at the "New Building" in New Windsor at noon on Saturday, March 15. What he did not reveal in the orders was that he himself would attend the meeting.

Ad copied the orders very carefully, but when he took them to the general for his signature, he could no longer maintain his silence. "Your Excellency, are you sure this is wise?"

Washington held up his hand, and Ad waited for a blast of temper to consume him, but instead, the general smiled at him with a rueful mixture of tenderness and exasperation. "My ever faithful Valencourt. How long it has been since first you tried to stay my folly."

Ad's skin heated with the memory of grabbing the bridle of his horse at Kip's Bay when the British were harrying them away from New York.

"Your Excellency, I had hoped you had forgotten that," he said.

Washington shook his head. "No, I do not forget those who would protect me at their own cost. Nor will I judge it amiss if you are not with me on Saturday. But I must be there."

"I would not abandon you so!" Ad exclaimed, so insulted by the suggestion that caution was forgotten.

"And I would not abandon my officers." The general's smile broadened with pleasure at winning the point.

Ad had surrendered, but while he was willing to risk his own skin, he was blunt with Matilda.

"I want you to be ready to go to Addie." Unspoken between them was the admission that if there were trouble, her brother, as one of Washington's Life Guards, would be no safer than Ad.

"Let me determine if I understand this." The calm of her voice was belied by the glitter of anger in her blue eyes. "The general will not leave his officers to their own destruction, and you and Luke will not forsake the general, but you expect me to flee if there is trouble. Just one more suggestion that I do so, and we will have the first grand battle of our marriage."

Ad opened his mouth to argue further and then thought better of it, conceding, "You share a most unfortunate trait with His Excellency in your refusal to be protected."

"Well matched with yours," Matilda insisted sweetly, but then all the challenge was gone from her. "Do you trust me?"

"With my life," he answered, though he did not understand the direction of her question.

"Then trust them. No matter their rage, the officers love the general as much as we do. They will not hurt him. To tear his flesh is to rend their own. They will not do that."

Reassured that the officers had cancelled their plan in order to comply with Washington's orders, and carrying Matilda's conviction with him, Ad, with other aides, accompanied the general on the fifteenth, though as soon as they were in the building, Ad hung back so as not to mar the general's progress with his own clumsy gait.

The appearance of the commander in chief in their midst brought a sudden silence to the crowd of officers and surprise showed on every face. He had their absolute attention when he started to read his speech from the paper he carried: "Gentlemen: By an anonymous summons, an attempt has been made to convene you together; how inconsistent with the rules of propriety! How unmilitary! And how subversive of all order and discipline, let the good sense of the army decide."

Having copied the speech, Ad knew the text, but he felt a start of alarm when Washington read haltingly and then stopped after the first paragraph. He saw why as His Excellency took out his spectacles and begged the indulgence of his audience as he put them on. "I have grown gray in your service," he said, "and now I find myself going blind."

He resumed reading, his attack on the writer of the anonymous paper unsparing. He suggested that it might be a plot engineered by the enemy in New York. He reminded the officers that his affection for them, for the army, was unquestionable.

Ad listened to the blunt eloquence of the speech, but he knew that the general did not need to read it; he had captured every heart when he had confessed his frailty and fumbled for his spectacles. Every face Ad could see reflected his emotions; many of the men were so moved, tears stood in their eyes.

When he had finished reading the last lines, the general left the officers to continue their meeting, left them to make strong avowals of their loyalty and patriotism.

"He may well have saved the country today," Ad told Matilda. "He is not only honorable himself, he expects to meet the same in others. I think that that expectation often creates the virtue." He drew a deep breath, but his voice shook in spite of his effort to keep it steady. "He touched us all today because he was telling the truth. I have been so reluctant to leave him, I have denied what is before me. He has grown old in our service. It is time for him to leave us. He deserves to go home to Mount Vernon. It is late to spare him much, but the sooner peace is made and all the enemy gone, the better."

Matilda held him close, cradling his head against her breast as if he were a child and not her tall, strong husband. In this he was a child, she knew, for no matter how Ad prepared himself for it, when the day came for him to bid the general farewell, it would be like losing his father all over again.

On April 11, due to news of the negotiations in Europe, Congress proclaimed a cessation of hostilities, and four days later ratified the preliminary treaty of peace that had been signed. A week later, Washington ordered that on the next day at noon cessation of hostilities between the United States and Great Britain should be announced to every regiment and corps of the Continental Army in and around the Newburgh headquarters.

As complicated and tedious as it was to make peace between governments so far apart in distance and in ideas, Ad gained enough confidence to write to Tench that he now had every hope that the general would be able to spend Christmas at his own home this year.

It was not the same as having Tench at headquarters, but his letters amused and pleased Ad. He was full of civilian, not military plans, particularly those regarding his wedding to take place in June. He was more sure than ever that Anna Maria had no equal among women, though he hastened to assure Ad that he knew Ad felt the same about Matilda. He was considering going into business in Baltimore as he thought the future of that town would be very favorable for trade, especially for the export of wheat to Europe. Ad was very flattered that Tench suggested he might want to be part of the venture, though he doubted he would be able to raise or borrow the capital required. Nonetheless, the offer intrigued him.

Everything changed for Ad at Dobb's Ferry in early May. He went with Washington's suite for a meeting with Sir Guy Carleton to work out details of the eventual British evacuation of New York and its environs. To his shock, Darius was with Carleton's party. Ad was glad to see his half-brother, though it was hard, too, because Darius looked so care-worn, much older than his forty years, and more like Marcus than ever.

But his face lighted with a smile the moment he saw Ad, and as soon as they could talk, he said, "I came because I expected you would be here," and he asked for news of Ad himself and of Justin and Addie, nodding in approval as Ad described their sister's success in Boston. Realizing how commonplace it had become to mention Johanna with her mother, Ad had to remind himself not to betray the secret to Darius.

"Addie is occupying the Summer Street house by herself?" Darius asked, thinking he had misunderstood.

"Yes," Ad said, with mental apologies to his lively niece.

"Then she must expect that you and your wife will join her soon." Darius sounded resigned, and much of the animation faded from his face.

Ad was confused by the change, but he answered as honestly as he could without mentioning his niece. "Addie would like that, yes, but that is not why she moved into the house. She wants a real home after so many years without one. I am not certain what Matilda and I will do. I have been in General Washington's service for so long, it is difficult to imagine civilian life."

Ad could see that his admission had cheered his brother before Darius asked, with renewed energy, "Will you hear me out?"

"Of course," Ad agreed, more curious by the minute.

"I did not come just to see you. I have a business proposal for you. After our losses in the Carolinas, it is the least I can do to see that those of my men who survived, and their families, are safely on their way from New York, and then I will leave, too. Some Loyalists may return someday, but I will not be among them." He did not have to explain to Ad that the organizer and leader of a Tory regiment that had warred against fellow citizens would not be welcome as long as Patriot memories lived.

"Settlements over lost and confiscated properties will be made eventually, but the squabbles between British and American authorities are likely to last for years. I would far rather that my interests in New York be placed in your hands. They are wholly mine, for I have long since discharged my debt to my father."

Very concisely he outlined the details that would make it profitable for both of them, with Ad buying him out over the years until in the end, Darius would have no interests left in New York. "It will be difficult at first, I know, but New York has a deep harbor for ships and is a fine port for trade with Europe. And now that Britain can no longer control it, commerce can only grow."

It was inevitable that Darius would be leaving, but Ad had not really thought too closely about it until now, and he felt an aching sorrow for him, for the love of place and regret at exile he heard in his voice.

"You trust me so much?" he asked, thinking of the possible consequences for Darius if he accepted the offer and could not perform the same miracle Addie was working in Boston. Like their father, Darius undoubtedly had some investments in England, but surely the bulk of his wealth was in New York. Along with a quickening interest in the deal, Ad felt an equal measure of fear at the idea of failing.

Darius brushed aside his trepidation. "Like our father in the last war, I profited greatly from contracts with the army early in the war. I supplied food, rum, fodder, draft animals, and other such items. I gave good value and was rewarded for my efforts, for all the good they did." He shrugged in acknowledgment of how futile it had all been. "You will not impoverish me if you suffer some reverses, but I would not suggest this did I not trust you. We may have had different mothers, but I believe we share our father's business acumen. Addie is proof of that, and she is your twin."

Ad admired Darius's attempt to be so positive about the situation when he so obviously wished he could play a part in the new age he foresaw for New York.

He could not resist asking, "Where will you go?"

"To England at first, but then I do not know. I doubt, for all my loyalty to the King and Parliament, that I am Englishman enough to stay there. Perhaps I shall go to the West Indies or to Canada. Many of us are settling there." His smile was a grimace. "It is fortunate for us that they were not lost, too."

Ad could not see him being happy in the warm indolence of the West Indies or in the Canadian wilderness, but he understood how Darius, American born as he was, and having spent most of his life here, would find England too confining on many levels. Darius loved America no less than Ad, but he had pledged to the past, mistaking it for the future, and now he would pay a high price for his fidelity.

"I must speak to Matilda about your offer, but we will consider it seriously, and I will send you word as soon as I can," Ad promised.

Washington's and Carleton's discussions went on for nearly a week, and though Ad's services as a secretary to the general kept him busy for long hours, he and Darius met when they could. Much of their talk was centered on business, for Darius's enterprises were complicated and had been made more so by the long years of British occupation and the ever increasing population of Loyalist and slave refugees, a population of thousands upon thousands who were quitting the town as fast as ships could be procured to take them away. Little had been done to repair the ravages of the fires of seven years ago or of the subsequent disasters, large and small, caused by having so many people crowded together in vile conditions.

Having gotten Ad interested in his offer, Darius seemed intent on painting as dark a portrait as possible until Ad protested, "Are you trying to discourage me?"

"No, it is to the advantage of both of us if you know the true conditions of the city when you make your decision."

But not all of their conversations were so dry. They did not say it, but they knew that there was little chance they would see each other again after this interlude ended. As Darius and Justin had last seen each other in the Carolinas, so Darius and Ad were marking their final contact. And thus, as if they were exchanging tokens of memory, they spoke of personal things and found much in common, though in the past the gap in their ages and their different mothers had made it seem as if they belonged to entirely different families.

As much as Ad pitied Darius for the exile he must endure, he envied him his closeness with their father and that he would see him soon. "You will tell Papa, please, that he is still and will always be close to our hearts, that he is never far from our thoughts? Had our cause failed, I know a reunion would have been possible, as well as I know that now it will never be."

Darius did not gainsay him, but in the course of their exchanges, Ad realized that while Marcus was lost to them, he, Addie, and Justin had each other, Matilda, Cordelia, the Castletons and the Freedoms, a vast family compared to Darius's isolation since his wife Harriet had died and his world had fallen apart along with British hopes of a victory. Darius was so hungry for news of even those he did not know personally, it was a constant temptation to add tales of Johanna's charm to the mix. Therefore, when Darius diffidently broached a "delicate matter," Ad listened avidly and willingly entered into the conspiracy.

On the last day of the conference between the powers, Washington went aboard the frigate that had carried Carleton up the Hudson. When he departed after dining with the British commander, there was a salute of seventeen guns befitting Washington's high military rank. Ad and his fellow aides fought to maintain their dignity when they felt like shouting aloud at this first complimentary salute by Great Britain to an officer of the United States. France, Spain, and Holland had officially recognized their independence, but in the thunder of British guns, the United States was at last a nation standing on its own.

As they left, Ad turned back to see Darius watching him from the deck of the ship. Simultaneously each raised a hand palm outward in private salute and farewell.

When Ad returned to her, Matilda listened to his account of the trip without interruption, and he saw his experience of sorrow and joy mirrored in her.

When he asked what she thought of Darius's offer, she answered obliquely, "Soon Luke will leave the army. He will go back to McKinnon. It is a place our father built, and it is much changed since he was killed. Nothing will be easy there. I fear for him, but it is right that he does this because he wants to, because he believes he can, because it does not matter to him that he will be building on our father's dream. He will make it his own. I do not question that you can make a success of New York; I know you can. But only you can know if you will be satisfied by doing so, by being your brother's agent at first."

She had gone to the heart of it. In America, far more than in Europe, there was the chance to begin new ventures. Marcus had done that. But Darius had built on their father's success, making it his own in New

York. Had the war never come, Ad believed he would have done the same, perhaps making Valencourt a recognized name in Philadelphia or elsewhere, while Justin succeeded their father in Boston. Taking over Darius's work in New York was but another variation of this progression, and Ad realized he wanted to do it.

Boston belonged to Addie now, and he did not want to return to that little seaport to live. But New York was another matter and a greater challenge. It might not recover from the rigors of war in his lifetime, but if it did, if its felicitous geography tipped the scales in its favor, then the possibilities seemed unlimited.

"I would be satisfied," Ad told Matilda. He smiled broadly. "Indeed I would!"

"Then New York it is, as soon as the minor problem of the British Army is removed," she said, her spirits rising. She was profoundly grateful to Darius, for now Ad had the practical solace of a challenge and definite work awaiting him at the end of his service to the general.

"We must tell Addie immediately," he said, though his smile wavered at the thought.

Matilda hastened to reassure him, repeating what Addie had said to her. "She will understand and be supportive of you." She hesitated. "However, she may not be so understanding about you and Darius interfering in her private life. Don't you think you ought to tell her about Colonel Traverne, too?"

"Probably, but I am not going to because there is nothing to tell her, really."

"It is a bit more than nothing that he is returning to this country," Matilda protested.

"He is coming back to see to his men. Darius did not know whether he plans to visit Addie or not, for all that he's asked about her in his letters."

Ad wished Darius had never broached the "delicate matter," for he felt as if he'd said too much and too little at the same time—allowing that his sister was fond of the Highlander, fond enough to have gone to Yorktown for the sight of him, but still not revealing Johanna's existence. But he suspected the worst thing he'd done was to tell

Darius that while it was difficult to fathom how the situation could be untangled, he and Justin respected Colonel Traverne as an honorable man and would not be averse to having him as a brother-in-law. This part of their conversation he had not related to Matilda, nor did he intend to. He felt as if he'd given a very inept performance as a matchmaker, and he cringed when he considered his twin's probable reaction did she know how her brothers were meddling in her life. But he tried to ease his conscience with the memory that he and Justin had also encouraged Silas, and for all the sorrow at the end, that match had been a good one.

"I don't want her to hope—or dread—that he will come to her when it is more probable he will arrive, complete his mission as swiftly as possible, and return to Scotland without ever going near Boston. It is, after all, none of our business," he insisted virtuously, wishing he'd remembered that when he'd been talking to Darius.

"You are right, of course," Matilda admitted. "But it is sad that Colonel Traverne doesn't even know he has a little girl, and that Johanna will never know her father."

Ad agreed, but he held on to his resolve when he wrote to Addie, making no mention of Traverne.

When Addie received the letter, her heart sank at this confirmation that Ad and Matilda would not be coming back to Boston to live, but almost immediately she saw the opportunity from Ad's point of view, and she rejoiced for him, understanding how much Darius's offer would assist in her twin's resumption of civilian life. And then she laughed at herself as her mind began to contemplate how good it would be for Valencourt interests in Boston to have a connection once again with those in New York. Business matters took up a good deal of her time and thoughts these days. Even keeping informed of the slow trudge toward a final treaty had commercial implications, for trade could not be normal until peace was fully restored. But it was more than that, and despite her distance from the scene her involvement was deep and personal.

She worried about Mistress Washington when Ad wrote that the lady had been somewhat frail of health, and as much as Ad, she wanted the Washingtons to be able to go home soon. She worried, too, about all the soldiers being furloughed out of the army, sent on their way down the road with no bands to play them out, most with very little to show for their faithful service, some paid in script for frontier lands they would never see, as they sold the paper to speculators as soon as they could in order to buy the meanest amounts of food and clothing. She thought of all the families she had met in the various encampments and wished she could know that they had gotten safely home. In particular, she hoped that Timothy Chepman, the boy whose life Silas had saved, would flourish as a man and would come to remember his commanding officer with gratitude untainted by guilt.

She was haunted by thoughts of the prisoners of both sides. At last they were being released. However, it was as complicated as everything else. She hoped Captain Trumble and his friends had long since been exchanged, but hundreds of Americans who had been held in the hulks were only now making their way home. It was extraordinary that they had survived at all, and their trials had not ended with their freedom. Gaunt, ill, possessing little beyond the rags they wore, many were reduced to begging for food as they struggled homeward.

Addie also worried about the enemy troops held by the Americans; she worried because of Iain's men, who had been marched hither and yon in the back country of Virginia, Maryland, and Pennsylvania. In this, though, the Americans did not have to bear the British burden of shame. While the prisoners held by the Americans had had their share of being cold, tired, hungry, and sick, with some deaths thinning their ranks, these conditions had been no more severe than those suffered by the American troops themselves and were not deliberately inflicted. Proof of the decent treatment they had received was in the great numbers of them, especially Hessians, who were deserting, deciding to stay in the United States, and were receiving permission to do so. American authorities had sent them deliberately into areas with significant German-speaking populations, and the ploy had worked. There the Hessians had not been viewed as monsters, and many had married into families who welcomed another strong back to help with the work. British regulars had deserted, too, though not as many as Hessians.

The thousands of enemy prisoners who remained loyal to the British were being brought north in various groups to the vicinity of New York, where, once back in the custody of their own army, they had little to do except wait on Staten Island or Long Island for the ships that would take them home. Among these, Addie was sure, would be every one of Iain's men who had survived. They were bound by their own code of honor and affection for each other, their regiment, and for Iain and his brother, the chief of their clan.

Too often, Addie wondered if her country could hold together long enough for the enemy to depart. In mid-June, Pennsylvanian troops at Lancaster mutinied, marched on Philadelphia, and persuaded the garrison there to join them in their demonstration before the Congress. As usual, the soldiers' grievances were valid, but Washington would have had little choice save to use his own troops to subdue the mutineers had they not laid down their arms and asked for clemency as suddenly as they had risen in revolt. Still, the alarm had been enough to send the Congress scurrying to Princeton, New Jersey, where they reconvened. The Congress was too aware that there was no money to pay the troops and that every day every soldier still under arms was a liability. Addie was thankful that Uncle Hartley had not had to endure the tumult; he had gone home at last. Though he might take his place in Virginia politics at some future date, for now he wanted nothing more than a quiet interlude at Castleton, a rest he had more than earned. Hart and Reeves were due home any time now, an event sure to cause days of celebration.

Addie had toyed with the idea of starting a newspaper to keep people apprised of political events, but with the news as dark as it was, she was relieved she had postponed that plan. Nor did she forget the trouble Marcus had caused for himself by expressing his political convictions through what he published in his paper. But the printing press was not idle. There were reprints to do whenever she managed to get new books from England, and there were all sorts of advertisements and public notices to publish. She had hired a skilled compositor and pressman and enough additional help so that she was not needed in the process, but she liked to check the proofs herself. The sound of the press, the acrid odor of ink, and the unique smell of the paper—all of it soothed her. She found that these familiar things conjured fond memories, not only of Silas, but of her father and brothers, of a time long ago. She was learning to accept that Silas as the man she had married was beyond her reach, lost with the man who had died in New York, but it was a comfort to remember him and the rest of them in childhood when Marcus had been the wisest man in the world, capable of keeping them from every harm.

She focused her thoughts and frowned at the advertisement she was reading. Then she laughed as she understood. "Mr. Tanner, 'bucks and eggs' seems an odd combination of items to sell," she said. "'Ducks and eggs' seems more likely."

"Yes, Mistress Bradwell, it is a 'd,' not a 'b' that's wanted," Mr. Tanner said stiffly. He believed in perfectly set type and did not find mistakes amusing.

"Perhaps there would be more interest in bucks and eggs?" Addie could not resist teasing.

Iain heard her laughter before he saw her, and when he beheld her face, golden eyes alight and an endearing smudge of ink across one cheek, he said her name, "Ariadne… Addie," and no more because his plan to approach her carefully, as nothing more than an old friend until he knew her feelings, was swept away by love, desire, and a tenderness so strong, he felt it as a blow.

Addie closed her eyes, but when she opened them, he was still standing there, and she asked his name in soft echo of his speaking hers. Then she said it again, no longer a question, "Iain!" and she went to him, compelled by the naked emotions on his face. She reached up and touched the long scar on his cheek and traced all the planes of brows, cheeks, nose, and mouth.

"I do not understand. How do you come to be here…? Why…?"

"Because you are here. Because I have missed you as if my heart were cut out. Because I could not stay away any longer. Because I know my life will be better spent here with you than in Scotland without you." He took out a handkerchief and scrubbed gently at the ink on her face. "Because you are beautiful even besmirched by the printer's trade. Because I would search the world over for 'bucks and eggs' if that is what you want. Because I love you."

He put his arms around her, drawing her close, and she rested her head against him, thinking she would gladly feel like this forever, thinking she had been waiting all this time for this impossibility, thinking—

The warmth turned cold as if the summer had frozen into winter in the blink of an eye. She damned herself for forgetting Johanna even so briefly, and yet, she could not sacrifice the contact with him.

Her voice was a dull whisper muffled against him. "My brothers, Ad or Justin or both, they have told you, or they betrayed me to Darius, who told you. However it was, you know, and you are here not for love, but for the duty I would have spared you."

When his body tensed, her worst fear was confirmed, and she fell so abruptly and so far into the darkness inside, she was still falling when his words began to make sense.

"I cannot see their sin, or mine. They did not give you to me in some medieval bargain. They did no more than assure me, through Darius, that they would not call me out for paying suit to you because they believe you have some feeling for me. Do you claim now that this is not true?" He was completely baffled by her lightning changes of mood, sure only that he had not misjudged her initial response to him.

Addie wanted to be angry at her brothers, to shift the blame else-where, but she could not when she thought of them trying so hard to do the best for her. Perversely, after all her warnings and threats to the contrary, she now wished they had told Iain about Johanna. Because they had not, she knew Iain was here for love of herself alone, but she thought she would have given up that knowledge to be released from the burden of telling him. She truly had not expected to see him again, and now the careful fiction of her life was to be revealed, and she could not predict the consequences.

"It is my sin, not yours," she said.

He held her away from him, looking down into her face. "I am too late? There is someone else?"

A last chance for a last lie; she could send him away with it. But she could not bear the look of weary defeat stealing over him.

"There is someone else, but not a man. You must come with me."

She led him from the printing office, and she realized the workers had moved away from the reunion to give the couple privacy, but it was too late; they knew Johanna well, and they saw her likeness in this man.

Beyond finally recognizing that they were heading toward the house where he had first met Addie, Iain's thoughts were as disordered as if he'd been spinning in place as he had done as a child, spinning round and round until the earth and sky kept racing even when he stopped, and there was no choice but to fall to the ground and wait for the universe to right itself. Darius had told him that Addie was living in the family home and that she had not remarried, but he had imparted few details of her domestic arrangements beyond that. Assuming that re-establishing Valencourt's in Boston would be taking most of her time, Iain had checked for her at the shops first, and only now did it strike him that the house was very big for her to be living in with naught but servants. Perhaps she was not alone. Perhaps there was a man after all. Perhaps. Thoughts going round and round.

When he and Addie reached the house, Iain was filled with the same sharp stir of blood and muscle that came right before a battle began. He could sense that whatever was coming would decide his future.

Once inside, they were greeted by a woman and child. Addie held out her hand to the little girl.

"Johanna, this is Colonel Traverne. Iain, this is my daughter, Johanna Bradwell."

The nursemaid faded away; the three of them were alone.

"Good day. I am almost three years old. Will you be my papa?" Johanna asked in her forthright manner, the question being a current favorite now that she had playmates and was aware of the normal configuration of families.

Iain looked into his own eyes in this tiny being's face, looked at a child who could have been one of his sisters when they were young, save for the subtle nuances of Addie in the shape of the eyes and mouth, a blending of blood that became more apparent with each second until, despite the black hair and blue eyes, he saw Addie as clearly as himself in Johanna.

The emotions came all at once, each more intense than any he had ever experienced before: rage that Addie had kept the knowledge of his child from him; terror that mother or child or both could easily have died in the birthing; gratitude that they had survived and that he was here with them; wonder that he and Addie had created such a miracle; desire for Addie even stronger than he had felt in New York; and love for both of them. The combined force brought him to his knees, and he bowed his head as tears burned his cheeks like fire.

Addie was paralyzed, her pain so great she jammed the knuckles of her hand against her teeth in an effort to hold back her cry.

But Johanna's attention was fixed on the man who had slumped to her level. She reached out and touched the scar on his cheek. "That's a big hurt. Did it make you fall down? Mama will kiss it and make it better."

Addie fought the hysterical laughter rising with her grief at Iain's pain—how to tell their daughter that not all kisses banished hurt, that sometimes they inflicted fatal wounds.

In battle, one action or the lack of it could decide between victory and defeat, life and death. In flashes of time too swift to measure, Iain had made such decisions countless times before, as he made this one, discounting all but the most vital information, knowing this battle was as important as any he had ever fought. Addie was not his enemy. She was his love, and evidence that she loved him in return was before him in their daughter, named for him. Addie had not had to keep the baby after having her. With the help of her family in Virginia, she could have kept the secret instead, fostered the child away, and returned to Boston with few the wiser.

"You are right," he told Johanna. "Your mama's kisses can make almost anything better." He put his arms around her very gently, and she showed no fear, wrapping her arms around his neck as he rose to his feet.

But when Johanna caught sight of the tears on her mother's face, her smile faded into puzzled distress. "Now Mama got a hurt, too."

"Then you and I will kiss her and make her better."

Addie's breath caught at the transformation in Iain. Rage, pain, and doubt were gone, taking years with them; love and his rejoicing in it were all that were left. Then she could not see for their closeness and for her weeping, but she felt Johanna's tiny kiss on one cheek and Iain's tender kiss on the other. The empty spaces were filled; the home she had sought to build for herself and Johanna was complete in Iain. Still her tears rained down as if in a deluge following a long drought.

"The kisses didn't make her better, and Mama never cries!" Johanna's voice quavered.

Iain said, "Sometimes big people cry when they are happy. Or maybe our kisses aren't as strong as your mama's, so we will have to give her more of them."

Johanna pursued this course with childish vigor, so that it felt to Addie as if a little bird were tapping on one cheek, but on the other, Iain's mouth moved with adult skill, tasting her skin, wooing her, making it seem as if that area were her whole body. She shivered at the sensation, and as Iain had intended, her tears stopped.

"You would teach her the art of ambush so early?" Her voice was husky from her weeping, but he heard the winsome tribute to his seduction, and the last coil of fear inside of him was gone.

"I would use any tactic to win her mother," he countered, and, still cradling Johanna with one arm, he drew Addie close with the other, binding the three of them together.

"Those kisses worked good!" Johanna chirped. "You gonna live with us now?"

"I am," Iain told her without hesitation, "but first I have to go away for a while to take some friends of mine back to their home. But after I have done that, I will come back to you and your mama. Will you wait for me?"

Johanna thought about this for a moment and nodded her agreement, but Addie knew the explanation and the question were for her. She could feel him waiting to know if she would understand.

"We will both wait," she said. His "friends" were hers as well—Angus, who had not survived to go home, Duncan and the others who had treated her so kindly. That Iain had come to see them home was fitting, even if it meant she must be parted from him once more. She had never hoped to have him with her again; to wait a while longer was small price to pay for the time to come.

"I heard about Angus. I am so sorry. But Duncan?"

"Duncan lives," Iain said. "Would that Angus did, too. I wish he could have known of our daughter. I am sure he would approve." Mentioning Angus brought Iain no sharp pain; the loss of him was a constant ache, like that from a severe wound long after it appeared to be healed.

A sudden horrifying thought struck Addie, and she could scarcely believe she had overlooked it until now. "It is all right for you to be here like this, out of uniform?"

Her mind darted from one plan to the next for hiding him or getting him safely away from Boston. Though he was in civilian clothes, he bore himself like a soldier, bore the scars of war, and her employees both here and at the shops would have seen this clearly, though she could not know what they might have made of it.

"Are you thinking of finding a gown large enough to fit me, to disguise me as a lady's maid? What an ugly woman I would make! It is not necessary. My exchange is complete, as is my resignation from the British Army. I have put down my sword for good, and I bear a passport recognized by both of our governments. See what sanction my courtship bears from such vast powers?"

It was a decision he had made, but she heard the lingering sorrow. He had been a soldier for most of his life, and the change would be great for him. It was ironic that this gave him much in common with many Continental officers and with her own spirit that missed army life. She would not miss it so much with him beside her and she hoped she could give him the same comfort.

There was much she wanted to know, but the first hours belonged to Johanna, and Addie marveled at Iain's patience with her. He admired favorite playthings and hiding places she showed him, talked about whatever subject she chose, and enthralled her with stories of a pack of adventurous children in the Scottish Highlands, "far, far away from here." And when Johanna had been fed, bathed, and put to bed with a final story, her parents stood together for a moment, simply watching her sleep.

"You are so good with her," Addie said when they had left her. "I would not have expected that."

"I have had some experience," he protested. "I have nieces and nephews. I spent a good deal of time with them these past months. And I was a child once myself; I did not spring from the womb with sword in hand."

"How fortunate for your mother that you did not."

"Minx." He kissed the tip of her nose, and she melted against him and felt tenderness turn to desire so swiftly in both of them, she was dizzy with it. His arms tightened around her, and he groaned, but then he held her away from his body. "No, not until we are married. I asked you before, and you refused. Now you must marry me to make an honest man of me." His tone was light to thwart the angry frustration that was making her eyes glow gold, but he was serious.

She capitulated because she understood it hurt him that Johanna had been born without the protection of his name. If he needed to do everything properly this time for the sake of his honor, then she would comply, but she muttered, "We must find someone to marry us very soon," startling a bark of laughter from him.

When he had decided to come to her, he had accepted that after so much time apart, at best there would be an initial awkwardness between them, and at worst there would be nothing left of the passion they had shared in New York, despite the recognition of it that had passed between them at Yorktown. He could not have imagined Johanna nor this feeling of familiarity he had with Addie, as if they had been together forever. He gloried in the warmth of it even as he acknowledged to himself that Addie and Johanna were so entwined in his heart, he would never again be complete without them. But while Addie had been patient, he knew she must have many questions, and he wanted her to know that he had not come to her devoid of prospects.

When he proposed it was time for them to talk, she agreed, suddenly greedy to know everything that had happened to him since Yorktown, though she knew the picture could never really be complete.

"When I returned to Scotland, I intended to stay there at least for a while, until it was time to take up my sword again. I was so weary those first days, I felt only relief to be home and that the lands my father forfeited for his brief loyalty to the Stuarts are returned to us."

He would not tell her that he had been ill, suffering from fever and the continuing effects of the wounds he had received at Guilford Court House. The scars he carried would forever remind him of Angus and of how that faithful man had risked and lost his life to save his.

"Then, as the time passed, I grew less and less content, and I did not feel as if I were home at all because you were not there. I told myself that there was no help for that, that it could not matter, but my heart would not listen. I began to view things differently. The Highlands are grand, as beautiful as any lands I will ever see. But they are more fit for beasts than men. The soil for planting and grazing is thin; the weather is harsh. The finest crop we produce is strong men and women, but the more there are, the less the land provides. The best work for many of the men is to go soldiering for whatever governments will hire them.

"For so long Rob and I have fought against losing our people, it has been difficult to admit that for many, it is better that they leave, far better than that they be left with little choice but to bear arms or starve.

"I knew before Yorktown that some of my men had, for all the violence they had found here, looked on your country and judged it fair and ripe with opportunities they will never have at home, no matter how much Rob strives to protect and nurture them." He paused, and his face was grave in the flickering candlelight of the drawing room whence all the soft last glow of the summer sunset had faded. "I want you to understand. To a man, my soldiers are loyal. They are not deserters, not traitors like many others who have decided to stay here. But they have refused to accept battle honors. Many came to feel they have more in common with Americans than with the government they were fighting for. And those who wish to stay are fearful that if they go back to Scotland, they will never be able to leave again.

"As you can imagine, communication has been slow and compli-cated. None are literate in their own language, but two of the younger men can read and write English, after a fashion, and the others had to rely on them to send word to me and Rob and then to translate our replies to them."

Addie thought of Angus's and Duncan's unease in the bookstore in New York, and she mourned anew for Angus.

"Though the letters were supposedly in English," Iain went on, "they were so labored and polite it took some care to understand what was being said. In the end, I think I understood because I was beginning to think as they were, and I told Rob so." He stopped again, thinking of what else he had told Rob, his confession that he was haunted day and night by the memory of an American woman.

"That must have been a shock to him," Addie said softly.

"Oh, yes, it was that, but Rob and I came to an agreement."

Iain had never seen Rob so angry. Rob had raged at him, calling him a madman, calling Addie a "wanton provincial" among other things, and then, finding English inadequate, he had started all over again, bellowing in Gaelic. For a long, dangerous moment, they had nearly come to blows. But Rob had looked at his younger brother's scarred, implacable face, and the fight had gone out of him, to be replaced by a sorrowful resignation that was harder for Iain to bear than his rage. Rob had gotten out his best whisky, rich with the smoky taste of peat, and the brothers had gotten drunk together, and Rob had decided he would be part of the process he could not fight.

"The matter of the regiment is a delicate one for your government and for Britain," Iain continued. "The best Rob and I can do for the men is to take them home with the promise that those who wish it may return here after the regiment has been officially disbanded and the final peace has been signed, which will be very soon now, I am sure of it. In that way, no charge of impropriety or lack of loyalty can be attached to them."

"And they will see their homeland and their families again, which may persuade some of them to stay there," Addie observed shrewdly.

"Yes, though Rob has more hope of that than I. By next spring, those men who wish it, and their families with them, will be back in this country. But those like Duncan who want nothing more than to live and die in the Highlands will stay home." It was another parting he would have to bear, but he was determined that Duncan believe that he had served Iain for long enough.

Addie closed her eyes at the thought of such a long separation, and Iain hastened to reassure her. "I will return before that, as soon as possible, by Christmas if I can manage it, or soon after, though I will have to spend time away from you once I am back here in order to arrange what I can for our people. They will settle, I think, in the western reaches of Maryland or Virginia or Pennsylvania—their time as prisoners has made them familiar with those areas." His tone was resigned rather than angry. "Some have gotten so familiar, I believe there will be a wedding here and there."

Compared to waiting until next spring, Christmas was close, and Addie counted the days, though she warned herself that fickle winds could delay the sailing going or coming. She was distracted by these inner calculations, but the sudden urgency in Iain's voice recaptured her attention.

"I do not want to fight any more, but it is what I am trained for. I cannot promise I will be successful without a sword in my hand, but I promise I will try. Timber, grain, tobacco, furs—there are commodities here that are wanted in Europe, and our people will not be the only ones who want transport to this country. Rob and I mean to be part of the traffic that will grow again once peace is restored. I will serve as the agent here, Rob there, and be damned to anyone who says we should starve in the Highlands rather than dirty our hands in trade! I do not mean to be your kept man."

"I have no doubt that you and Rob will be successful," Addie said calmly, but she had to clasp her hands tightly together to hide their shaking. It was so close, within her reach, but she had to be sure. "Will you mind that your wife also dirties her hands in trade?"

His surprise was genuine. "Of course not! In New York it was only that I did not want you to be so exposed to your enemies. I do not seek to tear down what you are building here, only to build something of my own for all of us." Then with a mixture of pride and apprehension, he started to ask a question of his own. "Here or anywhere we go, people will know that I am Johanna's father. Will—?"

She did not let him finish. "They will know what a fortunate child she is to have such a man for her father. I am a widow. Sometimes I catch a glimpse of Silas as a boy, but the man who was husband to me is gone. I will marry where I will, and I do not care how anyone else on earth judges it as long as it pleases you."

"It pleases me," he said, and she saw that he was shaking, too, and then he spoke in deliberate parallel. "In Scotland, I could see Jeane as a young girl, but the woman who was wife to me is gone. I will marry where I will."

They had been seated very properly apart, but when he opened his arms, she went to him and curled into his lap, and they clung to each other. They need never again regard each other as enemies, yet they had been faithful to their separate vows of loyalty, and the victory was shared, as were the sorrows, as the future would be.

Two days later, a magistrate performed the brief marriage ceremony. Addie had sent messages inviting a small number of people, including some employees and business associates and their spouses, to witness the event. They were people she respected and who treated her with respect, and she meant them to know that she was proud of Iain and of marrying him. But the blessing was in the presence of Tullia and Prince. She had sent her plea that they come, and had delayed a full day and night to give the Freedoms time to receive her invitation and to come to Boston if they would. Not until they appeared did she feel the day was complete.

Tullia looked into Iain's eyes for a long moment, and Iain looked back at her. Then Tullia nodded, saying, "You will take good care of her and your daughter," and Iain accepted the gift of her approval.

Addie wished the rest of her family could have been with them, and Iain's family, too, but it was enough that Tullia and Prince were there, and Johanna was happy that she had a guest of her own in little George. Addie knew some of the wedding guests would be discussing the odd mixture of witnesses and the overall strangeness of the occasion for some time to come. But they would also note the impression Iain made on them. Addie watched him charm them by his direct manner, treating each person as if he or she were deserving of his full attention. And for their part, the wedding guests seemed to accept him as a righteous man who had fought for his country but had now put down the sword he had raised against them. It was an indication of how ready for peace most people were.

Iain had requested one addition to the ceremony, and Addie had agreed because it was important to him. Johanna was thrilled to have a part to play and had listened very attentively and practiced at Iain's direction, though Addie had some misgivings about the laughter that had punctuated these rehearsals, not all of the mirth from their daughter.

Addie wore a light cloak over her gown while the magistrate spoke, and Iain stood beside her. But Johanna was concealed beneath the cloak. Addie could feel her pressed against her skirt, but the addition of an audience had silenced her giggles. When Iain and Addie had given the proper responses and the magistrate was finished, Addie pulled back her cloak, and Johanna peeked up at Iain, asking, "Now, Papa?"

"Now, kitten," he said. She came out of hiding and he swung her up into his arms, presenting her to the assemblage. "Our daughter, Johanna Bradwell Traverne."

Addie was touched and amused, and she could see their guests shared her feelings, some of the women wiping at tears as they smiled. It didn't matter whether they knew the origin of what they'd seen; the basic meaning was plain. But to Iain it was specific, a custom signifying that by Scottish law, though Johanna had been born illegitimate, she was not a child of adultery, and was now made legitimate by the marriage of her parents, her emergence from the cloak symbolizing that she was newly born to the marriage.

Addie loved seeing them together and hearing Johanna call him "Papa," and she loved Iain for being sure enough of himself and of her to insist that their little girl kept Bradwell as part of her name in tribute to a brave man who had sacrificed his life for his country.

"When she is old enough," Iain had told Addie, "we will tell her about him, and someday she will tell her children. Silas will not be forgotten."

Addie was resolved that when the time was right, she would show Johanna the few mementos she had of the war and tell her the story of each, of Paul Byrne's signet ring and the plain gold band she had worn as Silas's wife; of Quentin's artist's case kept safe by Matilda and Ad while she had been at Castleton; and of the blue eggshell fragment in which little Rand had seen such promise. She would tell her all of it and write it down so that there would be at least a chance that the objects would carry their histories with them through the generations.

The guests had been invited to partake of a wedding supper, and while Addie was pleased to see they were enjoying themselves, she could scarcely wait for them to depart. The Freedoms would be staying overnight, but that was all to the good, for Addie could trust them to keep Johanna occupied in the early morning when she was accustomed to seeing her mother. Addie had every intention of tarrying abed on the morrow.

When they were finally alone, Iain took her in his arms, raining kisses on her face and neck, nipping gently at her ears.

"It was a near thing," he murmured. "Had our guests stayed just a little longer, I would have proven myself the savage Highlander and carried you off."

"I was contemplating the same thing, though you are a trifle heavy for me to carry." She laughed at the image, her hands busy unfastening his clothing, as he began performing the same service for her. But her hands stilled and her laughter died when she saw the full extent of the scarring on his neck and chest.

The cut on his neck was a long continuation of the mark on his right cheek. The musket ball had hit him on the left side, the puckered scar midway between his shoulder and his flat nipple. Just a little difference and it would have hit his heart; just a little less luck and stamina; just a little hesitation by Angus in getting him away from the battle; and Iain would have died of the wound as it was.

"My love, so close, so close to losing you. I will be forever thankful to Angus for saving you." She was trembling, and there was so much pain on her face, as if she were feeling what he had when the wounds were fresh.

He could not bear it and drew her close again, gentling her with his hands and voice.

"Together we will remember Angus. But the danger is past. You did not lose me, nor I you." He stripped away the last of their clothing and picked her up, carrying her, after all, to the high bed.

Despite their hunger for each other, Addie's reaction to his wounds had moderated their pace, and they began to love with slow deliberation. Their bodies remembered each other. Iain could discern the subtle differences, the slight rounding of her hips and breasts; she was the same and yet forever changed by bearing his child. Addie touched the strength of him, the steely muscles over bone, the masculine contrast of smooth and furred skin. She felt his vulnerability, too; the flex of his body when she trailed kisses over his chest and with her hand traced the sinews of his belly and then the proof of his desire. She caressed him, inhaling the musky scent that was his alone.

Iain groaned, his control slipping away as he touched her as intimately and felt the wet heat of her. Murmuring to her in English and Gaelic, he moved over her and into her, and their bodies remembered and danced together as if the music had never stopped.

When they quieted, still twined together, but at rest, it came to Addie that being with him now was so much more than it had been. There was no guilt in this, no tortured ghosts and open graves waiting when she closed her eyes. She felt the security of their marriage wrapped around her and their daughter like the wedding cloak, transforming them into a family. It would be hard to see Iain leave them even for a short time, but it would not rend the new weave of their lives.

She lay with her head on his chest, close to his heart, and she felt as much as heard his words.

"Nothing on earth could have kept me from you tonight, but I hope I did not get you with child. I would that I be with you this time."

"I hope I do conceive. It would be good for Johanna to have a brother or sister soon, before there are too many years between them." She thought of Callista and Darius, who had always seemed so far away by age until she had come to know Darius as an adult. "It takes some time, you know. If you do not dawdle in Scotland, you would be back in time to see me at my most ungainly, or to make sure I am so 'ere long. You mustn't worry. My life was all turmoil then, but I had no trouble bearing Johanna." Someday she might tell him that she had cried out for him during the birthing, but not now when he needed reassurance for the fear she heard in his voice.

"Thank God for it," he growled, his body stirring, "for not even my best intentions can keep me from this," and the dance began again.

They tried to pretend they had endless time, but the truth added a sharper edge to their passion than their newly wedded state. They would have but three nights together before Iain must leave. His men waited on Staten Island for the ship that would carry them away, and he could not miss the scheduled sailing.

The days were no less precious, but they belonged to the three of them, to Addie and Iain and Johanna. It was such a short time to explore all the joys of being a family, but they did their best, and Johanna was so proud of having acquired a father and so pleased with his attention, she did not seem to mind that her mother was distracted. When Addie showed Iain the various Valencourt enterprises, both of them had to hide their smiles at Johanna's earnest contributions. At one warehouse, she informed her father, "Big boats come with lots of boxes and things to go in there, but I am not ever, ever to go by myself 'cause those boxes can fall on me. But I been in here before when Mama took me." She drew a deep breath. "I like this smell!"

Iain smelled the same bouquet—the blend of sea, rope, tar, and old, damp wood mixed with spices, coffee, fruit, and myriad other scents. He sniffed noisily and exclaimed, "I do, too!"

"Mama don't always like it," Johanna confided. "Sometimes she looks like this." She clenched her small face in apt imitation.

Addie blushed and protested, "It's the tar."

Iain laughed, but beneath his laughter his heart ached at the realization of how alone Addie had been, so alone that a very young child had been her closest companion in both her business and domestic lives. He could not and would not change either of them; they were strong and had survived for him to come to them, but he would do his best to show them that they did not have to rely on themselves alone anymore.

He hoisted Johanna onto his shoulders and caught Addie's hand in his own. "Let us explore and see if we can name everything here by the smell of it."

"When you sniff out the rats, do not identify them, please!" Addie hissed in his ear, but she was laughing, and she looked so young and carefree, his breath caught and he had to look away.

At night when their bodies were satiated, they defied sleep, anxious to make the most of their time, talking for hours. But they were not heedless young lovers compelled to tell everything. There were questions they did not ask, answers they did not give. Addie wondered if Iain suspected she had spied for the Americans. In some ways, it would be easier to admit she had, to blunt the power of the truth to wound at some future date. But the secret was not hers alone, and so she kept silent.

And part of Iain wanted to confess to her that he had not been faithful to her after he had returned to Scotland. He had thought to forget her, but he had searched for her in every woman and had bedded the few who bore some small resemblance to her. He had been resigned to never seeing Addie again. He had forced no one, promised nothing, and still he felt as if he had broken vows to Addie and wished he could be absolved by her. But to obtain absolution would mean hurting her with his honesty, and so he kept silent.

They did not shy away from every difficult subject. They spoke of Darius with mutual affection, and Addie had reassured Iain, "I do not believe Ad or Justin told him about Johanna. I do not think he knows of her existence. He is your close friend; he would have told you." She did not have to explain that that was exactly why she had demanded the news be kept from him.

Darius had been on the point of leaving New York when Iain had arrived, and the men had had time for only the briefest of meetings, a circumstance that had made Darius less tactful than usual.

"Addie seems to have some interest in you, according to her other brothers. If it is mutual, I suggest you see her while you are here."

He'd shaken his head. "As if there were not enough confusion in our family." But there had been no rancor in his voice, and he had not asked for any details nor if Iain would act on his advice.

"You should be the one to write to Darius about our daughter," Addie paused, "or will you go to see him and the rest of the family... my father..."

They were lying side by side in the dark, candles long since guttered down, but he did not need the light to see the sorrow in her. While he was home, he had gone to England to see Marcus Valencourt and the others, including Callista, who had referred him to her father's house in Boston all those years ago. It had been a cordial reunion, but a sad, uncomfortable one, too. Iain had described the visit as kindly as he could to Addie, but there was no way to soften her father's intractability.

Marcus had aged greatly during his exile from America, and even after Yorktown he had still believed that it was not possible for Britain to lose the war. And though his soul was torn by the harm and grief that had come to Lily's children, he remained unrelenting in his belief that they were traitors and that the victory they had helped to win would bring ruination to their country.

Now he said, "I will send them word of our marriage and of Johanna, but I will not go to see them. There will be no time for that, but more, I fear I could not be civil again to your father. I can imagine that Johanna may someday do something of which I will not approve, but I cannot imagine that I would ever abandon her as your father has you and your brothers."

Addie started to protest, ready to defend Marcus as always, but Iain stopped her by asking, "And you, could you abandon Johanna?" He raised her hand to his mouth and kissed her fingers and palm, soothing her, though he knew nothing could ever entirely ease the pain her father had caused. "There is another reason I will not go. I feel too much pity for Darius, and he would know were we face to face. I may come and live in the United States, and my men, too, but Darius cannot, nor can thousands of Highlanders who once lived in the Carolinas, Georgia, and elsewhere, and have now fled. I understand it—a stranger who fights against you may be forgiven; a neighbor or a friend who does the same is condemned forever—but it is harsh."

"And we are very fortunate," she whispered, shivering though the night was warm. There were so many things that should have kept them apart. She interlaced her fingers with his in sudden urgency, and his touch changed, too, slipping out of her grip only to begin stroking each of her fingers in turn, summoning passion again from so small a point of contact.

They held fiercely to each other, but they could not hold back the hours, and in the morning, it was time for him to go.

For Johanna's sake, Addie did not cry, and for the same reason, Iain made himself smile as he told their daughter once more that he would be with them again soon. He kissed them both, embraced them, and then released them.

Addie murmured, "Keep safe. I love you."

And even after the coach had rolled out of sight, Johanna kept waving and saying, "Bye-bye, Papa, bye-bye."

Chapter 8

New York City, Fall 1783

Late in August at the request of the Congress, the Washingtons had moved to the Berrien House at Rocky Hill outside of Princeton, New Jersey. None of the headquarters staff had looked forward to the disruption, but the countryside had turned out to express their affection as the commander in chief and his lady passed by, and Princeton had proved pleasant, particularly for Martha, whose health had improved in the spacious farmhouse. With the Congress in session in Princeton, social life was lively and offered some diversion from the boredom of waiting for final word of treaty negotiations to come from Paris.

There was increasing anticipation of the return to civilian life, and now Ad shared it because there was so much to be done in New York once he could go there. But the undercurrent of sadness persisted as more and more troops were discharged and the military life they had all known for so long faded away. In October, Washington issued his last general order to the Continental Army. In it he expressed his pride and gratitude in the army's endurance that "through almost every possible suffering and discouragement, for the space of eight long years, was little short of a miracle." At the same time, Congress declared that from November 3 onward, all those soldiers who had been previously furloughed were "absolutely discharged," thus furthering the army's extinction.

In late October, they had news of the treaty's arrival in New York. This was the final version signed in Paris by representatives of Great Britain, the United States, France, Spain, and the Netherlands in early September. There was no question that Congress would formally ratify it in the coming months.

They waited now for the last act of the enemy, for Sir Guy Carleton to complete the evacuation of New York. True to his word, he had made every provision for Loyalists like Darius to leave for Canada, the British West Indies, and Great Britain. From spring through summer and into the autumn, the harbor had bristled with the masts of vessels, large and small, being used for transport. American as well as foreign craft had been hired. In addition to the Loyalists, there were the thousands of military prisoners, such as Traverne's men, who had been released by the Americans and needed to be shipped home. It was a massive undertaking, the removal of virtually a large city's population in a matter of months. Last to go would be the troops on active duty.

Because of his twin's marriage, Ad saw the treaty and evacuation through her eyes as well as his own, and he exulted that there was no further impediment to her husband's return.

Before Colonel Traverne had passed back through British lines to New York, he had gone out of his way and had requested a meeting with Ad. With Washington's permission, Ad had agreed. The meeting had taken place before Ad had received his sister's letter, but he had been relieved rather than shocked at Traverne's announcement of their marriage.

Traverne had described his and his brother's plans, but then he had said, "We will do our utmost, but there are so many uncertainties, I cannot promise we will be successful. I can promise that I love Addie and Johanna and will until I die and that I will do the best I can for them, always." He had looked away for a moment, and then he had asked, "Colonel Valencourt, Darius was not mistaken that you and your brother Justin have some sympathy for this match?"

Despite his civilian clothes, everything about the man—from his scarred face to the sheer power of his presence—had reminded Ad of what a formidable enemy he had been, and of what a valuable ally he could be. Ad had realized he did not like having him humble before him.

"Darius was not mistaken, nor are you. Johanna is proof enough to us that Addie loves you. We want our sister's happiness as much as our own, and she has found it in you. You are sacrificing much to be with her."

"It is quite the opposite," Traverne had insisted. "Addie sacrificed much to bear our daughter, and I believe we can have a good life in this country. However, I do not mean to offend, but I have some misgivings about the future governance of this nation. You have defeated the British, a remarkable accomplishment, but I am not sure what you have won. I worry that my wife and child will be more endangered by civil discord than by disease or accident."

It had been plain to Ad that there was no mockery in the man; he had been genuinely curious and uneasy, and Ad had responded honestly, accepting as Traverne did that what currently passed for the government—a Congress long since proven powerless even to force the states to contribute the monies needed to pay the army, let alone other debts—could not support the costs and complications of establishing a strong country. And with the war over, the necessity of cooperation between the states for the sake of defeating a common enemy no longer existed.

"We are no more certain than you of what we will become," Ad had said. "But we have won more than victory over Britain. We have won independence and with it the right to choose what kind of nation we will be, for good or evil. I am not the only one who understands that independence without order is anarchy, and anarchy the worst tyranny. There are enough of us so that I believe we have at least a chance of choosing a just course, free of kings and dictators, and there are few citizens in the history of mankind who have had that."

"You and your sister are twins, indeed, for all the blessed differences between you. And if, after hazarding so much, you are willing to gamble on, then I can do no less." Traverne had smiled, reminding Ad so forcibly of Johanna, he had understood how it was for the man to see Addie in him and Justin.

As they parted, Ad had said, "A swift, safe journey, Colonel Traverne."

"Please, my name is Iain."

"Ad," he had offered in return.

Ad had not missed the significance of the Highlander giving his Gaelic name, rather than what the English made of it, and in that small exchange and the relinquishing of military titles and formality, he had felt as if they had signed their own treaty.

He related the news of the marriage to the Washingtons with an edge of defiance, though he did not feel obliged to include Johanna's parentage.

He need not have worried.

The General had considered the matter and then nodded: "Far better to have such a man with us than against us. We could use more like him in the years ahead."

"I am so glad for your sister's sake!" Martha had exclaimed. "Addie is dear to me, and I have not liked to think of her being a widow for so long. I have good proof that second marriages have great merit." She had smiled so fondly at her husband, Ad had wanted more than ever for the Washingtons to be able to be home together by Christmas.

Now months later, in November, it seemed more possible, though it would be a near thing for the general. Martha was home, and trunks of her husband's papers and most of his other belongings had been packed up and sent to Virginia, as if in promise that he would soon follow.

Ad and the few other remaining aides had found it difficult to say goodbye to Martha, the brave woman who had traveled north every winter to cheer the general and to make headquarters seem like a home. It was hard for her, too, but she had had special words for each of them.

To Ad, she had said, "I refuse to believe we will not see you soon at Mount Vernon. Now that you are to be an uncle again, you and Matilda must surely travel to Virginia when the baby arrives." As she had intended, she had made him smile at this reminder of the news that Justin and Cordelia were expecting their first child; other news she had kept to herself. But she had added very softly, "Thank you, my dear, for taking such good care of the general for so long. A little more time, and then send him home to me."

Ad had not allowed himself to dwell on the truth that with all there was to be done in New York, it would be years, if ever, before he could go south again, despite all the ties of blood and friendship he had to Virginia.

Martha had insisted on saying a private goodbye to Matilda, and that night, Matilda had wept disconsolately in Ad's arms.

"I hate this! I don't want to say farewell to any more people!" Her sorrow was double, for her brother had just left, too, heading back to the frontier to begin rebuilding McKinnon. Matilda had known the date of his departure for weeks in advance, but that had not eased the reality of being separated from him.

Ad and Luke had had their own emotions to deal with, and they had done so with a minimum of words.

Ad saying, "I will take care of her."

And Luke replying, "I know you will."

Thinking of both Mistress Washington and Luke, Matilda had snuggled closer to Ad, stopping her crying with an audible effort. "Just hold me. As long as I don't have to see you go away, I can bear anything."

"Never, my love. We are going to grow very, very old together." He had drawn as much comfort from her as he gave.

After Mistress Washington's departure they had left Princeton, heading for West Point where General Knox was in command of what remained of the Continental Army. An early snowstorm delayed their progress for three days, but they had reached their destination without further mishap and with time to spare.

At West Point, final arrangements had been made with Sir Guy Carleton for him to evacuate New York and for Washington to enter the city on the same day. Now they waited at Day's Tavern at Harlem, nine miles from the city as British pickets withdrew and Continental pickets advanced to take over one outpost after another. Ad and Matilda had found a room in a farmhouse close to the tavern. It was plain, but adequate, and Matilda pointed out that it was much better than being exposed to the elements or to the overcrowding at the tavern.

The night before they were to leave, she announced she was not going with the army into New York.

"I will await you here."

"You've come this far, why not the last small distance?" Ad protested.

"Because this is the finish of your service to the army and to the general, and I don't want you distracted from it. When you return, your resignation from your commission will be official, and you will be a soldier no more. But I will be waiting." Her smile was at once soft and sly. "We will be waiting." She touched her still flat belly. "I give you the news to take with you, to remind you that this is as much a beginning as an end."

He was unable to make a sound at first, and then he heard himself asking all the questions, as if in a litany fashioned long ago. "Are you sure? Are you well? When will it come?"

To which Matilda answered, "I am sure, and so was Mistress Washington. She guessed." She giggled at his expression of dismay for not having done the same. "She has far more practical experience than you or I," she reminded him, "and I have betrayed myself in some way that Addie did not. Probably because I am not so complicated a person as she is. I am well and strong, and the baby will arrive in May, I think."

Ad kept shaking his head and repeating, "How could I not have known? How could I not have noticed the changes?"

Matilda was still amused and bursting with the joy of sharing her secret, but she sought to soothe his distress. "These have been trying months. At first, I thought nothing of the changes either. But never, in all these days, have I felt neglected by you."

The full wonder of it caught up with him, rushing through him in tangible warmth, and he hugged her close. "My sweet, sweet Matilda," he murmured, and they laughed and cried together. When he could draw breath, he said, "We Valencourts are certainly doing our best to provide new citizens for this new nation. And with Hart and Reeves home, and by Justin's account being entertained by all the eligible women for miles around, I expect there will be weddings soon and young Castletons, too—I hope in that order!"

Matilda stilled in his arms. "I know Addie will be happy for us, but I am sorry she is not carrying a child, too. She wrote to me that she is disappointed that she did not conceive a brother or a sister for Johanna while Iain was with her."

"Well, I am not disappointed. Far better that Colonel—Iain—be back before that happens. And I have no doubt that it will."

The mixture of resignation and admiration in his voice amused Matilda anew. "Highland garb is not proscribed here; surely when he returns, Traverne will not limit himself to breeches or trews. You would present an exceptionally fine figure in a kilt," she purred. "You would be so accessible to me." Despite her best efforts, laughter undermined the husky suggestion.

"As to every passing breeze! Spare me from bawdy women!" Ad's prim tone was belied by his roving hands.

He left the next morning armored with all the joy Matilda had given him for defense against the waiting sorrow. Not the least of those joys was the fact that Matilda, of all people, knew how marked and misshapen his lame leg was, but it had so little significance for her, she could tease him about wearing a kilt.

He felt whole and strong as he rode off with Washington's suite. Though cold, the day was brilliantly clear. General Knox commanded the American troops who would take possession of the city, and they were for some time so close to the British rearguard, the American and British officers chatted back and forth quite cordially. In order to prevent the pillaging and rioting Carleton feared, there was to be no lapse of time between one army leaving and the other coming in, and patrols and guards organized by the citizens had protected the city during the previous night. But the populace seemed more inclined to cheer than to run amok.

The American force of a corps of dragoons, one of artillery, some battalions of light infantry, and a rearguard under Knox followed close behind the British until their paths diverged at Wall Street, with the enemy turning on Pearl Street to march on toward the water and the boats assembled there, while the Americans proceeded to Broadway. At Bowling Green, General Knox collected the body of mounted citizens who had gathered there and led them out the Bowery to the Bull's Head Tavern, where Washington's party and that of George Clinton, Governor of New York—and no relation of Sir Henry Clinton—had assembled and were waiting. Compliments and congratulations were

exchanged all around, and then the procession formed to escort
Washington and Clinton into the city.

Washington, on his gray horse, and Clinton, their aides, and a body
of Westchester Light Horse were at the head of the column, followed
by other state officials, then Knox with his officers, then the mounted
citizens, then the Speaker of the Assembly, and last, citizens on foot. The
Continental troops had done the best they could to make themselves
presentable in their worn uniforms, and the citizens sported sprigs of
laurel in their hats and a "Union" cockade of black and white ribbons
on the left breast of their shirts or coats; the device had been designed
a few years before in celebration of the French Alliance. The officers
of the army and the citizens marched eight abreast, and crowds lined
the way to cheer and in many cases to call out to soldiers, relatives,
and friends from whom they had been separated since the British
occupation of the city.

Ad felt his own swell of emotion. Seven long years it had been
since they had been chased out of this city, seven years since Quentin
had been killed on Long Island, four years since Silas had died here,
months since Darius had sailed away into exile, and now because of
the massive evacuation, what had been the last Loyalist stronghold
was becoming a city of Patriots.

Even while the troops fired a salute, and a reception at Cape's
Tavern got underway, the last of the British were embarking to leave
the city entirely in American hands. There would be enemy soldiers
on Staten Island and Long Island for some days to come, as they
awaited transportation, but any threat from them was gone, as they
were gone from the city.

New York threw itself into a delirious round of receptions and
celebrations, and Ad and the other aides scarcely had time to draw
breath as they escorted the general from one function to the next.
There were some odd visits Washington insisted on making, and
he explained little aside from warning Ad and the other officer who
accompanied him that nothing was ever to be said of this business.

Ad quickly realized that the general, directed by Colonel Tallmadge, was conveying his personal thanks to spies who had served

the American cause. There was a tailor, a tavern keeper, and a few other tradespeople, but to Ad, the shock was the inclusion of James Rivington, infamous Loyalist and royal printer during the British occupation of the city. Ad worried that it would be suspicious that a man as well known as Rivington had not departed with other Loyalists, but then, no one believed that every Tory had fled.

Rivington had recognized Ad immediately, and they had exchanged polite greetings, with Rivington saying, "Darius told me of your arrangement before he left. I hope you will prosper as he did."

They visited him at his printing establishment and from a private office with the door ajar, Ad heard the telltale clink of coins while Washington had an interview with Rivington. Whatever the man had done, it was worthy of a tangible reward at a time when coins were still in extremely short supply.

Later, as Washington's little party was quitting the premises, Rivington said softly to Ad, "Please extend my best wishes to Ariadne."

It seemed innocent enough, after all Rivington had known their father and them before the war, but his dark eyes were alight with what Ad could only term mischief, and in that instant Ad knew that Addie had had some contact with the man while she was in New York, spying on the enemy.

"I will," he answered courteously, but he shuddered inwardly at the risks Addie had taken, and he hated the idea that she had dealt with someone like Rivington, who had spread such lies about the general.

Rivington seemed a most unlikely Patriot. Perhaps he had just seen much earlier than his fellow Loyalists that the Americans were going to win. Though the visit from the general would bespeak special favor and should protect Rivington from the most extreme Patriots, even while it would enrage them, the cause of the visit could not be divulged and so he could not depend on spying to enhance his position in civilian life. The necessity of spying did not make it respected. Addie never spoke of it to Ad; he did not expect she ever would; and he doubted that Rivington, despite Washington's visit, would have an easy time of it with the British gone.

When Ad could manage a little respite from duty, he used it to check on Darius's properties. There was damage here and there, but his brother had done his best to protect everything as well as he could. At Darius's request, officers on Sir Guy's staff had occupied the house these past months, thus having comfortable quarters while keeping the house intact, and it was a tribute to Darius that they had held him in high enough esteem to comply with his wishes even to the end, and not plundering the house when they left.

This was not the only precaution Darius had taken. He had hired watchmen, but more, he had posted every site with plaques that read: "This is the Property of Lt. Colonel Darius Valencourt, Valencourt's Rangers, and of Lt. Colonel Adrian Valencourt, Aide-de-Camp to General George Washington, Continental Army."

Ad smiled in rueful appreciation when he read the first sign. What better way to give notice that there was no political justification for either Loyalists or Patriots to pillage the holdings? He was also moved to see his name linked with his half-brother's; it strengthened his determination to make the transition of ownership from Darius to him work.

He had no illusions about how hard the work would be. Despite the festivities, the city had a desolate air. With Sir Guy's permission, many of the Patriots who had quit the city in the wake of the British occupation had returned as the Loyalists left. The city was by no means empty, but it showed the effects of having supported too large a population. Trees, fences, parts of buildings—anything that could provide firewood for heat and cooking—had disappeared, and the older ruins from the conflagration seven years ago added to the picture of neglect. Dead weeds choked old gardens, and rubbish lay in heaps.

Part of the population who had left had been the slaves who had fled to the British. Sir Guy had kept his promise to them, too. Though there were rumors that some had been sold in the West Indies, there were reliable reports that others had been taken to freedom in Nova Scotia. Ad had promised his sister that he would search for Josiah and the other slaves who had left Castleton with Benedict Arnold and that he would aid them if he could. But the chance for that was gone. While one by one the Northern and Middle states were beginning to abolish slavery, the Southern states showed no inclination to follow their lead. The best Ad could hope for Josiah and his companions was that they had survived, and that wherever they were, they were free.

Ad missed Matilda even after so short a time of being away from her, but he decided it was just as well she had not come into the city when it was so unsettled and he could not be with her constantly. He contented himself with sending her messages, which was not difficult with the traffic flowing in and out. The excitement in New York would fade with the general's departure; time then to bring Matilda in for a close inspection of their properties.

Every time Ad thought of the general leaving, his mind flinched away, and yet he was conscious of the minutes ticking past. The other aides and officers close to the general were equally aware, and for them the victory celebrations were tinged with melancholy. In spite of his restraint, it was clear the general felt it, too.

The Congress, which had still not settled on a permanent meeting place, had, at Maryland's invitation, moved to Annapolis. Washington, accompanied by General von Steuben and a few aides whose homes lay to the south, was to travel to Annapolis, where he would appear before the Congress to officially tender his resignation as Commander in Chief of the Continental Army. But for Ad and other officers, their close, private journey with His Excellency and with each other would end in the Long Room of Fraunces Tavern at the corner of Broad and Pearl Streets. December 4 was their final day together, and it was also the day that saw the last of the British ships weighing anchor and dropping down the bay, bound for England.

Their first night in New York had been spent at a great dinner given at the tavern by Governor Clinton, with Washington and many of his officers among the huge crowd. But this dinner was different. Only the general and those few officers who remained in the city were present.

There was food set out, but no one had any appetite. The general filled his glass with wine, and he toasted his officers.

"With a heart full of love and gratitude I now take leave of you; I most devoutly wish that your latter days may be as prosperous and happy as your former ones have been glorious and honorable."

Ad fought for control, wanting to weep like a child. Then he realized he was not alone. The men wept without shame. At that moment, it ceased to matter that some of these men wanted the general to be crowned king, that others wanted a military dictatorship to rule the country, and that Washington despised both of these alternatives.

His Excellency, his own control broken, voice thick with tears, said, "I cannot come to each of you, but shall be obliged if each of you will come and take me by the hand."

General Knox, who was closest to Washington, turned to him, and both of them wept as they embraced without words, and so it went, with each coming to the general. Ad had no words, either, and tears were rolling unchecked down his cheeks when his turn came. He held out his hand, the general grasped it, embraced and kissed him as he had each of the others. When Ad stepped back, he saw such grief on his commander's face, his own heart twisted with physical pain. He and the others were paying tribute to the general for his leadership through so many hard campaigns to this impossible victory, but most of all, they came to him because they loved him and knew he loved them no less. With all the personal plans they had made, none of them could truly imagine what they were going to do without him and without each other. It was as if they were losing their commander in chief, their fathers, their brothers, and their closest friends all at once.

Ad left the tavern with others of the staff to perform a last small service for His Excellency, following as part of his escort as he went to join Governor Clinton and city officials. Once more composed, and magnificent in his blue-and-buff uniform, the general took his formal leave, passing through a line of light infantry to the Whitehall Ferry where a barge waited to take him to Paulus Hook on the Jersey shore. When he, von Steuben, and the others were aboard, the barge pulled away, and good wishes rang out across the water. The General waved his hat in acknowledgment, and that was all.

Ad stood there for a long time, watching the barge and figures on it grow smaller, waves of anguish passing through him, countless memories of his eight years with the general flashing before his eyes.

Then, suddenly, Matilda was there in his mind's eye, as she had been when he first saw her, as she was now, just a short distance away, waiting patiently for him, with their child curled inside her. Matilda understanding him, believing in him, loving him.

Though he knew the general could neither see nor hear him, he raised his hand in a last gesture of farewell and whispered, "Godspeed."

The General had done his part and more. If all went well, he would be home for Christmas and for days and years of peace to follow. Now it was up to the rest of them to hold fast to the independence they had won at such cost and to create from it a nation worthy of that sacrifice.

Ad turned his back on the water, away from the past. He would be with the future, with Matilda, before dark.

Historical Note on
Principal Real-Life Characters

BENEDICT ARNOLD (1741–1801) was never brought to trial in the United States, and the British government provided adequately for him and his family. However, the very treachery that had made Arnold valuable to the British also made him distasteful to them, and he was not accorded the respect, the accolades, nor the riches he expected in England, so perhaps there was some justice done for his treason. Nor was he successful in his business ventures, including a sojourn in Canada. Benedict died in 1801, Peggy in 1804. They were buried in an unremarkable church in London, on the south side of the Thames.

HENRY CLINTON (1738–1795) spent a great deal of time, effort, and ink in trying to prove that it was not his fault that the war in America had been lost, but since the British government and public needed a target, Sir Henry's protestations were to little avail. In spite of this, his reputation was gradually restored to the point that when he died, he was serving as Governor of Gibraltar.

CHARLES CORNWALLIS (1738–1805) was not blamed for losing the war—Clinton was scapegoat enough for that. Cornwallis went on to serve his government well as Governor General and Commander in Chief in India, as Lord Lieutenant of Ireland, and as Plenipotentiary to France. He had been sent to India again when he died there.

NATHANAEL GREENE (1742–1786) died in Georgia at the age of forty-four. South Carolina and Georgia had given him land for his valiant leadership of the Southern Campaign. But in the course of that duty, he had suffered severe financial setbacks. When the Congress had proven unwilling and unable to support the troops in the South in the closing years of the war, General Greene had pledged his own honor and property to financiers in order to supply his men with the basic necessities. Unscrupulous middlemen in the deal ruined his credit and, as a result, he had to sell much of what he owned. His struggles to recoup his family's financial security surely contributed to his death, the immediate cause of which seems to have been a combination of overwork and sunstroke. His wife Kitty (1755–1814) was only thirty when Nathanael died, and the eldest of their five children was only twelve. Ten years later, Kitty married Phineas Miller, who had been with the family since 1783 as the children's tutor. Kitty and Phineas are best remembered for their association with Eli Whitney; it was they who led him to invent the cotton gin.

ALEXANDER HAMILTON (1755–1804) was a key figure in getting the Constitution ratified and served as the first Secretary of the Treasury under the Constitution. A passionate advocate of a strong central government, he was the leader of the Federalist party and an enemy, both personally and politically, of Thomas Jefferson, the leader of the Democratic-Republican party. Despite this, Hamilton threw his support to Jefferson in the 1800 presidential election in order to ensure the defeat of Aaron Burr, whom Hamilton detested and mistrusted. In 1804, when Burr sought the governorship of New York, Hamilton again helped to defeat him, denouncing him harshly. After the election, Burr demanded satisfaction; Hamilton refused to retract his words; Burr then challenged him to a duel. It is a sad irony that Hamilton, who had never approved of dueling and who had lost a son to the tradition a few years before, felt compelled by his public stature to accept the challenge. The duel took place on July 11, 1804. Hamilton made no attempt to aim his weapon, and he died the following day from the wound inflicted by Burr. His wife Betsey (1757–1854) survived Alexander by fifty years.

HENRY KNOX (1750–1806) served as Secretary of War under the Articles of Confederation, and when Washington was elected president, Knox retained his office under the new Constitution. He retired from federal life in 1794 and spent much of his remaining time at his estate, Montpelier, Thomaston, Maine, though he, Lucy, and their brood visited Boston and elsewhere when their finances allowed. Lucy (1756–1824) in particular liked the social life cities offered, and she was delighted when Henry was elected to the Massachusetts legislature (Maine then being under that state's jurisdiction), since that necessitated travel to London even when their purse could not easily afford it. Though he seems to have been forgotten in the present age, Henry was a popular figure in his own time, and Lucy was described as a formidable, attractive woman to the end of her days.

MARIE JOSEPH PAUL YVES ROCH GILBERT MOTTER, MARQUIS DE LAFAYETTE, (1757–1834) returned to the United States in 1784. He was given a grand welcome by the country, and he spent joyful days visiting with the Washingtons at Mount Vernon. Lafayette and the general did not see each other again, but they corresponded until Washington's death. Though Lafayette believed in certain liberal principles and in a Constitution, he remained a monarchist. Nonetheless, he survived the French Revolution and five years of imprisonment by Austrians and Prussians. It seems he even came to genuinely love his ever faithful and often neglected wife, Adrienne. Lafayette visited the United States once more, arriving in New York City on July 12, 1824, for a fifteen-month tour of the states. While many of his old comrades were gone, the country still remembered him with immense gratitude and affection. He was seventy-seven years old when he died in Paris.

HENRY ("LIGHT HORSE HARRY") LEE (1756–1818) was never as successful as a civilian as he had been as a soldier, though he served in Congress and as Governor of Virginia. He was regularly inept in financial matters. Nor was the course of his personal life smooth. His first marriage, to his cousin Matilda Lee, was a love match, but she died in 1790. Three years later, he married Ann Hill Carter. The fifth child of this marriage was Robert E. Lee, who would become the commanding general of the Confederate Army. Injured in a riot in Baltimore in 1812, Harry spent his last years as an impoverished invalid, wandering the West Indies in search of better health. His friends, James Madison and James Monroe, raised the money to enable him to travel there. However, his health continued to decline, and at last, sensing that death was near, he tried to get back to his family in Alexandria, Virginia. He made it only as far as Cumberland Island, Georgia, to Dungeness, the home of two of Nathanael and Kitty Greene's daughters and their families. Though a frail old man, to the Greenes' descendants he was still Light Horse Harry Lee, hero of the Revolution, and so he was also to soldiers and sailors stationed in the region. At their own request and considering it a privilege, these young men took turns keeping vigil day and night at his bedside until Harry died a few weeks after his arrival at Dungeness.

FRIEDRICH WILHELM LUDOLF GERHARD AUGUSTIN STEUBEN'S (1730–1794) claim to the "von" indicating nobility and to the title of "baron" were of doubtful validity, but certainly he demonstrated his worth in his service to the Continental Army. After the war, he was granted American citizenship as well as land and a pension.

BANASTRE TARLETON (1754–1833), whose name had become a synonym for savage butchery in the United States, returned to England, where he lived long and was successful in political, military, and civilian life. He never felt the slightest remorse for his conduct in America; rather, his *History of the Campaigns of 1780 and 1781 in the Southern Provinces of North America* boasted of his exploits.

TENCH TILGHMAN (1744–1786) died only three years after the final peace had been signed. He was only forty-two years old, but his health had remained fragile after he left the army. At the time of his death, he and Anna Maria (1755–1843) had a daughter, and another daughter was born six months later. Tench had stayed in close contact with the Washingtons, and they and many others who loved him mourned his passing. Anna Maria lived until 1843, but she never remarried.

THE WASHINGTONS' return to country life was short-lived. In 1787, George (1732–1799) was the presiding officer at the convention held to revise the Articles of Confederation. And when the Constitution established the new nation, he was the obvious—the only—choice for first president of the United States of America. He served two terms, declining a third. He gave his farewell address in September 1796 and returned with Martha (1731–1802) to their beloved Mount Vernon. Three years later, he died, his death undoubtedly hastened by the barbaric medical treatments employed by his physicians in their attempts to cure his dangerously inflamed throat. Three years after George's death, Martha died. In him and in her, during the war and forever after, the new nation was truly blessed.

Made in the USA
Monee, IL
26 November 2024

71319640R00111